Christy Jeffries graduated from the University of California, Irvine, with a degree in criminology, and received her Juris Doctor from California Western School of Law. But drafting court documents and working in law enforcement was merely an apprenticeship for her current career in the dynamic fields of mummyhood and romance writing. She lives in Southern California with her patient husband, two energetic sons and one sassy grandmother. Follow her online at www.christyjeffries.com.

To my Monkey Roo. Your superfast race-car brain has been such a blessing and continues to amaze me every day. You are so smart, creative and incredibly witty. Even though I can't wait to see what kind of man you'll grow up to become, you will always be my little boy. I love being your mommy.

"Wait. Why am I explaining all this to you?" Julia asked.

"Because I have the kind of face that makes people want to open up?" Why was he being so damn flirty? It was as if Kane couldn't stop the asinine comments from flying out. But she'd caught him off guard looking like that. Plus, she was much more down-to-earth when she rambled on about nothing.

"No. You have the kind of face that makes people feel as if they're strapped to a polygraph machine." That was an interesting revelation. Did he make her nervous?

"You don't like my face?" He reached up to stroke his famous trademark beard, then remembered he'd shaved it several months ago when he'd moved to Sugar Falls. Instead, he touched a bristly jawline that felt like eighty-grade sandpaper.

"I'm not going to answer that, either." But he could tell by the blush rising up from her scoop-neck tank that she probably liked his face more than she wanted to admit.

* * *

Sugar Falls, Idaho:
Your destination for true love!

THE MAKEOVER PRESCRIPTION

BY
CHRISTY JEFFRIES

First Published in Great Britain 2017
By Mills & Boon, an imprint of HarperCollins*Publishers*
1 London Bridge Street, London, SE1 9GF

ISBN: 978-0-263-92270-7

23-0117

Chapter One

Captain Julia Calhoun Fitzgerald had no problem commanding a full surgical team in the operating room during an emergency decompressive craniectomy, but she could be naked, standing on her head and yelling from a bullhorn, and nobody in the Cowgirl Up Café would give her a second look.

"May I get some…" Julia's voice trailed off when she realized she was talking to the back of the busboy's turquoise T-shirt. He'd unceremoniously dropped the plate of food off on the counter between her seat and the empty one next to her, not bothering to ask if she had everything she needed.

She looked down the counter and saw an unused place setting two seats over. She could either sit here, going unnoticed for another twenty minutes—which was how long it'd taken for the waitress to take her order in the first place—or she could reach over and grab the neighboring paper napkin and utensils. She decided to do the latter.

After centering the newly acquired napkin in her lap, Julia neatly cut her oversize breakfast burrito in half with surgical precision, then clamped her lips shut at what looked to be sausage gravy oozing out of the center. This couldn't be right. She lifted her head and looked around the restaurant, hoping to catch the attention of the lone waitress who was darting between several crowded tables, fumbling with her order pad before picking up a stack of dirty plates from an empty table.

Was this place always so crowded? Since being stationed at the Shadowview Military Hospital last month, Julia had come into her aunt's restaurant only twice, and both times were right before closing when most of the small town of Sugar Falls, Idaho, shut down for the night.

And speaking of Aunt Freckles, where was she anyway? Julia could've sworn the calendar app on her fancy new smartphone said they were supposed to meet at the café at eight this morning.

She glanced at her gold tank watch—one of the more modest pieces she'd inherited from her mother—and noted that she had only about fifteen minutes before she was supposed to meet the contractor at her new house.

Julia used her fork and knife to probe at the contents of the flour tortilla on her plate, then leaned forward and sniffed at the batter-covered meat inside. This was definitely not what she'd ordered. She carefully set her utensils down on either side of her plate and took a sip of her orange juice while observing the other customers and trying not to eavesdrop on the intense conversation going on in the booth to her right.

"There's no way the Rockies are going to make it to the play-offs this year, let alone win the pennant." One of the older-looking cowboys slammed his fist on the table, making the salt and pepper shakers rattle as the equally elderly man beside him nodded in agreement. "And if you try to tell me their bull pen is stronger than the Rangers', I'll call you a liar."

Julia squirmed in her seat, trying not to listen to the heated discussion but unable to tear her gaze away.

"Now settle down, Jonesy," said the younger man sitting on the opposite side of the booth. He was holding up his hands, the sleeves of his gray flannel shirt rolled up to reveal strong, tan forearms that could only be the result of years of outdoor physical labor. His short auburn hair was messy—probably due to the green hat precariously hanging on his bouncing knee—and his square jaw and smirking lips made Julia's pulse want to do the opposite of settle down. Luckily, though, his quiet voice, or maybe his overall size, had the proper effect on Jonesy, who took a couple of deep breaths before nodding. Sexy Flannel Shirt continued, "Nobody said anything about their pitchers. All I said was..."

Out of the corner of her eye, she saw the server approach, and Julia turned away from the conversation, slightly lifting her hand in an attempt to get Monica's attention. At least, she thought the name tag read Monica. She couldn't be sure since the woman kept passing by in a blur, not even glancing in Julia's direction.

"Excuse me." Julia tried again when Monica rushed behind her side of the counter, this time balancing three plates of food in one hand and a carafe of coffee and a bottle of syrup in the other. But the young woman still didn't look her way.

Sighing, Julia decided that she'd settle for eating what she could off the plate. She hated being late, and since the contractor was a good friend of her aunt's, Julia wanted to make a good impression. She picked up her fork and began eating the home fries, which she had to admit were delicious, if a little greasier than her usual breakfast fare. Just as she swallowed the last bit of potatoes, she heard a choking sound coming from the booth beside her.

Sexy Flannel Shirt had his hand covering his mouth, and Julia sprang into rescue mode. Within four strides, she'd pulled the man out of the booth and wrapped her arms around his torso, locking them in place directly above his upper abdomen. His chin almost collided with her forehead when he whipped his head back quickly to look at her.

"You'll be okay," she said in her most authoritative tone. "Try to stay calm."

"I would be a hell of a lot calmer if I knew why you were latching onto me like that," the man replied. If he was capable of speaking, he was capable of breathing.

Oh no.

Julia rose awkwardly to her full height, her hands disengaging so slowly, she could feel the softness of his flannel shirt under her fingers. And the tightness of the muscles underneath. Obviously her senses were on high alert because of the quick adrenaline rush she got whenever she was in an emergency situation like this. Even if it was a false alarm.

She quickly clasped her overly sensitive hands behind her back.

"Sorry," she said to Mr. Flannel, as well as to the two older cowboys sitting with him at the table, their eyes as large and round as their stacks of blueberry pancakes. "I thought you were choking."

"I thought so, too," the man admitted. "Then I just realized that I was being poisoned by whatever was inside my chicken-fried steak burrito."

He pointed to his plate, and Julia suddenly realized where her breakfast order had ended up.

"It looks like you got my egg white and veggie delight wrap." She picked up the plate and walked back to her seat at the counter, then returned with his meal, the spilled gravy not yet congealing. "I think I got yours by mistake."

"What happened to my hash browns?" he asked, looking at the empty space alongside his burrito.

A defensive heat rose up from the neckline of Julia's hospital scrubs, all the way to her hairline. Who put chicken-fried steak in a tortilla, anyway? "I, uh, ate them when I realized that the burrito wasn't what I ordered."

"Most people would've just sent the order back if it was wrong," he said, his lips twitching, giving her the impression that he found her mistake hilarious.

Oh really? She wanted to ask. *They wouldn't gasp and choke and pretend to be poisoned?* But she didn't know this man, or the rest of the people in this town. Yet. And Julia didn't want to start off on the wrong foot with her new neighbors. Although she had a feeling that with all the eyes—including Monica's, *finally*—in the suddenly quiet restaurant staring at her, she'd already made quite an impression.

The pressure on her sternum felt as if someone were trying to save *her* from choking…on her own embarrassment and she had to silence the whispers of one of the other few times she'd been so foolish. She returned to her seat and picked her leather satchel up off the floor, retrieving her wallet out of the front pocket before walking back to his booth.

"Here. This should cover the cost of your breakfast." Julia's voice wobbled as she pulled two twenty dollar bills out, setting them on his table. Then, before she walked out the door, she decided someone had better tell him.

"And just so you know, there's a piece of spinach stuck in your teeth."

Julia dodged the waitress and her tray full of food as she made her way to the front door. Several shouts of laughter reached her ears right as she exited, but she didn't pause or turn back to see who was making fun of her. Instead, she squared her shoulders and walked down the sidewalk of Snowflake Boulevard, wondering how long it would take for news of the embarrassing scene she'd just caused to make its way down the shops and businesses lined up along this main road through town.

This was why she was more comfortable in the background. Out of the way. Being ignored.

She'd just climbed in her car when her cell phone chirped to life. Seeing her aunt's name on the display screen, Julia quickly answered it.

"Sug, where are you?" Aunt Freckles asked.

"I just left the café." No need to tell the woman about how she'd accosted one of the customers by mistakenly performing the Heimlich maneuver. Her aunt would probably find out soon enough, anyway.

"Why would you go there?"

"Because we were supposed to meet there at eight."

"No, we weren't. We were supposed to meet at the bakery. Why would I have you come to my restaurant when I'd already taken the morning off?"

Well, that would explain why the café was so understaffed. But how could Julia have gotten the location wrong? She tried to tap on her calendar app to confirm that she hadn't screwed up twice this morning, but she accidentally ended the call. Ugh. She squeezed the phone in frustration, then took a deep breath and reminded herself that she was smarter than this. She tried to pull up Freckles's number, but before she could find the right button, a text message from her aunt popped up saying they could just meet at the new house, so Julia put her MINI Cooper in gear.

Turning onto her street, Julia gazed up at the ramshackle old Victorian that stood at the end of the cul-de-sac on Pinecone Court, a proud smile making her cheeks stretch and alleviating her lingering shame over that awkward encounter just a few moments ago. If one didn't count the Federal-style mansion in Georgetown, the summer cottage on Chincoteague Island in Virginia or the countless commercial properties still held in the Fitzgerald Family Trust, Julia had never owned her own house.

She parked her car in the driveway, biting her lip and staring out the window, trying to envision all the possibilities spread out before her. Unlike Julia, this house was anything but practical and understated. But all thirty-two hundred square feet of it was hers.

There were no interior designers to suggest beige color palettes and overpriced modern art. No maids to rush in and make up her bed the moment she'd robotically woken up at five thirty every morning to practice the cello. No private tutors waiting in the informal library—the formal library in the Georgetown residence being reserved for when Mother invited her university colleagues over—to ensure Julia's MCAT score was high enough. After all, they needed the med school admission counselors to overlook the fact that she wasn't old enough to buy liquor, let alone cut open cadavers to research the long-term effects of liver disease. And there was no personal chef here to tell her that her parents had already instructed him on the week's menu, so she would *not* be eating processed carbs for dinner, no matter how many of her classmates were cramming for finals over pizza and Red Bull energy drinks.

A horn blasted behind her, and she turned to see her elderly Aunt Freckles behind the wheel of a slightly less elderly rusted-out 4x4 that Julia didn't recognize. Freckles was actually her great-aunt on her father's side, and while Julia only had sporadic contact with her relative until her parents' joint memorial service several years ago, it didn't take a neurosurgeon to figure out why the flashy waitress and former rodeo queen had been estranged from their conservative and academic family.

"Morning, Sug," Freckles hollered—there was really no other way to describe the woman's cheerfully brash voice—as she patted the Bronco emblem near the driver's-side door. "Ain't she a beaut? My second husband, Earl Larry, had one just like it back in '73. We hitched an Airstream to it and cruised all over Mexico."

She brushed her aunt's weathered and heavily rouged cheek with a soft kiss as Freckles wrapped her in a bear hug that threatened to crush several ribs. Julia was still accustoming herself to the woman's hearty displays of affection. "Whatever happened to Earl Larry?" she asked, always interested in hearing about her aunt's series of past relationships.

"His grandpappy died and left the family business to him. Earl Larry went corporate on me, and after that *Forbes* report came out with him on the cover, I told him I wasn't made for that kind of life. I couldn't stand being married to some stuffy old three-piece suit, no matter how many capital ventures he sank our RVing money into."

It was hard to imagine anyone named Earl Larry wearing a suit, let alone having a grandpappy who left him a company that would be featured in a well-respected financial magazine. Of course, it was just as difficult to imagine seventy-eight-year-old Eugenia Josephine Brighton Fitzgerald of the Virginia Fitzgeralds wearing orange cowboy boots, zebra-printed spandex pants and an off-the-shoulder turquoise T-shirt emblazoned with the words Cowgirl Up Café—We'll Butter Your Biscuit.

"Whose car is this?" Julia asked.

"It's Kane's," Freckles said. "I saw him pulled over on Snowflake Boulevard, and he said he'd eaten something that hadn't agreed with him. I told him he just needed some fresh air, and since I've been itching to take this old Bronco of his for a spin, he agreed to let me drive it so he could walk the rest of the way. It's only a couple of blocks, so he should be here any sec."

Julia had yet to meet Kane Chatterson, the contractor Aunt Freckles suggested she hire to remodel the house. But if this derelict hunk of junk on wheels was any indication of the man's rehab skills, her once-stately Victorian abode was in serious trouble.

Of course, if her overzealous impromptu CPR skills back at the restaurant were any indication, Julia's medical career as a Navy surgeon might be in serious trouble, as well.

"Would you like to see the inside of the house?" Julia asked.

"You bet," Freckles said in her mountain drawl.

"I have only an hour before my shift at Shadowview, so I might ask you to give Mr. Chatterson the tour if he isn't here soon. I can email him some of my notes and suggestions later."

What Julia didn't say was that it would certainly be a load off her mind if she could just skip all this formal meet and greet business and fire off a quick note to the guy. Especially after the disastrous morning she'd already had. But Aunt Freckles's quick shake of her dyed and teased peach-colored hairdo was enough to suggest Julia shouldn't keep her fingers crossed.

"Kane's a good boy and dependable as sin. He'll get here in time. Besides, I'm holding his baby ransom." Freckles dangled the metal keys above her head. "And men have an unnatural attachment to their cars. If you ever took the time to go out on a date with a decent fella, you'd find that out for yourself."

Julia rolled her eyes, a practice that she never would've dared in the presence of her parents when they'd been alive. But, seriously. Her aunt referred to every male under the age of sixty as a boy and never missed an opportunity to suggest Julia's social life was too date-free—at least by the older woman's standards. Freckles liked men almost as much as she liked sequins and comfort food.

"I'm in and out of surgery all day, and when I do get the occasional time free, I usually spend it swimming laps or sleeping at the officers' quarters near the base hospital."

"You work too hard, Sug," Freckles said, rubbing her niece's shoulder. Julia, who normally tried to remain as reserved as possible, had difficulty not leaning in to the comforting motion. "And you gotta eat sometime. In those blue hospital scrubs and that cardigan, you look like you haven't got a curve to your name. Isn't there a nice doctor or admiral or someone you could go out to dinner with?"

"I don't need a man to take me to dinner."

"Hmph." Had her aunt just snorted? "I don't know if I mentioned this yet, but the town of Sugar Falls puts on a big to-do at the end of the year to raise money for the hospital. Since you're one of the new surgeons and an official resident of Sugar Falls, the committee is going to expect you to be there as a guest of honor. With a plus-one, if you know what I'm saying?"

Guest of honor? A plus-one? Julia's stomach twisted and her forehead grew damp, despite the fact that the early November sun still hadn't peeked out of the clouds. She was pretty sure her aunt was suggesting she'd need to find a date, which was much easier said than done. Besides, Julia never wanted to show her face in the town of Sugar Falls again.

"Oh, look," Freckles continued. "Here comes Kane now. Smile and try not to look so dang serious."

Julia's insides felt tighter than a newly strung cello as she turned around to await the contractor who would be doing the remodeling work on her new home—if his estimate was reasonable. Yet before she could formulate her plan to refrain from shoveling out piles of her inheritance to someone in order to avoid the hassle of negotiating, she recognized the familiar gray flannel shirt, and her heart dropped.

Oh no. Please, no. This can't be happening to me.

The man hadn't seemed quite as tall when he'd been sitting in that booth back at the Cowgirl Up Café, but his broad shoulders and chest looked just as muscular as they'd felt twenty minutes ago. He moved with long, purposeful strides that ate up the sidewalk, and Julia didn't know whether she should meet him halfway and beg him not to mention the choking incident to Freckles, or whether she should hide in the overgrown azalea bush.

In the end, she was too mortified to do either. Her aunt motioned the man up the uneven cement path and onto the porch. "Kane Chatterson, meet my favorite grand-niece, Dr. and Captain Julia Fitzgerald."

The pride in her aunt's voice blossomed inside Julia's

chest, nearly shadowing the lingering shame. Or was that just her elevated heartbeat?

"I'm your *only* niece," Julia said, trying to lighten things up with a joke, but she succeeded only in making her nerves feel more weighed down. She cleared her throat and looked at Kane. "We weren't formally introduced earlier."

God, she hoped this man didn't spill the beans to her aunt. His sunglasses shaded his eyes, and he certainly wasn't smirking now, making it impossible for Julia to figure out if he was annoyed, amused or biding his time until Freckles left and he could tell her that she and her contracting job weren't worth the trouble.

But Kane Chatterson simply gave her a brief, unsmiling nod before asking, "Do I call you Doctor or Captain?"

"Call me just Julia. Please." She reached out her hand to shake his, and he gripped her fingers quickly, his warm calluses leaving an imprint on her palms. As a medical professional, she had no rational or scientific explanation for the shiver that vibrated down her spine. As a woman, her only explanation was that this new sensation was most likely the result of her aunt's fresh lecture on dating. And possibly the fact that she hadn't been this attracted to a man since...ever.

"Just Julia," he replied. But still no smile.

She looked at her watch. She'd be out of here in ten minutes. Surely, she could pretend to be a normal, successful woman for another ten minutes.

"What do you mean, you weren't formally introduced earlier?" Damn. Aunt Freckles didn't miss a thing.

"We, uh, spoke briefly at the Cowgirl Up Café when our orders got mixed up this morning," Kane told her aunt. The faint dusting of copper-colored stubble on his square jaw made it too difficult to tell if the man was actually blushing.

"Yeah, I figured the new waitress I hired wasn't quite ready for me to leave her on her own," Freckles replied, then turned to Julia and gave her a wink. "Seems like lots of people are getting stuff wrong this morning."

"Here." Julia handed the cell phone to her aunt, determined to prove that she hadn't made a mistake. Or at least two of them. "It says right here on my calendar app that we were supposed to meet at the café."

Since Freckles was busy tapping on the screen and Mr. Chatterson's attention was on the yellow paint chipping off the wood siding of the house, Julia stole another look at his dour face. She'd been trying to save his life back at the café. Surely he couldn't be irritated with her over that—unless the laughter she'd heard as she left the restaurant was directed at him. Maybe the guy's ego had taken a hit. Or maybe his feet were cold and tired from walking all this way from the restaurant.

Julia glanced down at the scuffed cowboy boots. No, that sturdy, worn leather looked like they'd been walked in quite a lot. So his stiff demeanor most likely wasn't the result of sore feet. She allowed her gaze to travel up his jeans-clad legs, past his untucked shirt and all the way to his green cap with the words Patterson's Dairy embroidered in yellow on the front.

That funny tingling made its way down her spine again.

What was wrong with her? She didn't stare at unsuspecting men or allow her body to get all jumbled full of hormones, no matter how good-looking they were. Julia reached up and tightened the elastic band in her hair, hoping he wouldn't look over and catch her checking him out.

"Sug," Aunt Freckles said, holding up the smartphone.

"Somehow you managed to program the Cowgirl Up Café as the location for everything in your calendar this month—including five surgeries, two staff meetings, a seminar on neurological disorders and the Boise Philharmonic's String Quintet."

"Oh. Well, I haven't had time to go over the new software update. Yet." Julia waved her hand dismissively before powering off her screen. That wasn't a real mistake. She had much more important things to accomplish than mastering some stupid scheduling app—like getting this tour underway if she wanted to report for duty on time. She pulled a key from the pocket of her cardigan sweater, the one Aunt Freckles said did nothing for her coloring or her figure, and asked Mr. Chatterson, "Would you like me to show you around inside?"

"I could probably figure it out on my own," he said, then used the top step to wipe his boots as she unlocked the door. "But it wouldn't hurt for you to tell me some of your ideas for the place."

Well, wasn't he being generous?

"Shouldn't you grab a notepad?" Julia gestured toward his run-down truck-vehicle thing.

"Why?"

"So that you can take notes?"

"Don't need to."

"What about measurements? Surely you won't be able to remember every little dimension."

"No, ma'am. I probably won't. In fact, there's probably a lot of stuff I won't remember. But I'll get a sense of the house and what it needs, which is something no tape measure can show me."

"But how will you give me an estimate?"

"*If* I decide to take the job," he said, looking up at the large trees, their pine needles creeping toward the roof she was positive needed replacing, "I'll come back and take measurements and write it all down neat and tidy for you."

"Sug," Freckles interrupted in a stage whisper. "Kane here knows what he's doing. He doesn't come into the operating room and tell you where to cut or how to dig around in someone's brain." Then, as if to lessen the rebuke, Freckles turned to the brooding contractor. "Julia's a neurosurgeon in the Navy. Smart as a whip, my grandniece. Did I mention that?"

"I believe you did. Should we get started?" he asked, wiping his hand across his mouth. Then, without waiting for a response, he walked through the door as though he couldn't care less about Julia's abilities in the operating room or her whip-like intelligence. Not that she wanted the attention or expected him to be in awe of her, but it was one of the few times somebody hadn't been impressed with her genius IQ.

The guy strode into her front parlor as though he owned the place, and Julia resented his take-charge attitude and her unexplainable physical response to him. However, he was the expert—supposedly—and she was intelligent enough to know that this old house needed much more than her surgical skills.

The trio made their way from room to room, and Julia lost track of the amount of times she had to tell Aunt Freckles that she didn't love the idea of glitter-infused paint on the walls or a wet bar added to each of the three floors. When they finished the tour in the kitchen, Julia was already in jeopardy of being ten minutes late for her shift. Unfortunately, she didn't trust her aunt not to suggest something outlandish in her absence.

"I say you get some of those cool retro turquoise appliances and redo all these cabinets with pink and white paint." Freckles waved her arms like an air traffic controller. "Then you can do black-and-white-checkered tile and give it a real fifties' vibe. If you knock out this wall, it will open up the kitchen to the family room."

"Which room is the family room?" Julia rubbed at her temples before tightening her ponytail. Again.

"I believe that's the room you referred to as the study," Kane told her. His smirk gave off the impression that he was laughing at her for some reason. Again. "Or was that the informal parlor?"

"Either way," Julia said. "I don't want a fifties-themed anything in my house. Besides, remodeling the kitchen is my last concern."

It was difficult to not startle at Freckle's loud, indrawn breath. "Sug, no, no, no. The kitchen is the *heart* of the house. That should be the first thing Kane works on. How're you gonna cook or eat if you don't have a decent kitchen?"

"I don't intend to do much cooking here. I eat most of my meals at the hospital, and as long as I have a refrigerator to store all the leftovers you give me, I should be just fine."

The woman tipped her head back, then rubbed her fingers over her eyes. Julia feared her aunt was going to smear her purple eye shadow. "It's just that with the Pumpkin Pie Parade coming up and then ski season right after, I'm going to be so busy at the café. I worry about you being all alone, not eating right and withering away to nothing."

"I assure you, I value my health too much to allow myself to wither away," Julia said. "But I know you worry about me, and if it makes you feel any better, I'll buy a cookbook and teach myself some basic recipes. After all, how hard can it be?"

"Sug, I know most things come easy to you," Freckles said, wrapping her thin arm around Julia's waist. "But there're a lot of things in life you just can't learn from a book."

Unfortunately Julia knew the truth of that statement all too well. Freckles was her last living relative and the reason Julia had transferred duty stations and moved to Idaho. If it would ease the woman's mind to know that her only niece would have a fully functional kitchen, then Julia would give Sexy Flannel Shirt permission to start tearing out the old rotting cupboards today.

Julia leaned into Freckles's one-armed embrace. She didn't even have to look at the contractor's estimate to know that no matter how absurdly high his price might be, she would end up hiring him just to appease the affectionate woman.

"Fine," Julia said. "First things first, though. I need my bedroom to be in habitable condition. Then Mr. Chatterson can start on the kitchen. But no turquoise appliances or checkered floors. All design ideas need to be approved by me."

"Of course, Sug."

"Now I *really* need to get to the hospital," Julia said, glancing at her watch. "Take your time looking around."

"You want me to lock up afterward?" Kane asked after she hugged her aunt goodbye.

"That would be great, if you don't mind. Do I need to sign anything?"

"Not until I send you the estimate. Like I said, I haven't decided if this project is something that will fit into my schedule yet."

Julia collected her leather satchel on her way to the front parlor, then glanced out of the glass-paned entryway toward his old car parked in her driveway. His schedule was probably chock-full of appointments involving lots of smirking and consultations on how to give strangers the silent treatment. Unfortunately for her, that kind of work likely didn't pay his bills. Which meant she'd be stuck convincing herself that she could easily handle this unexpected attraction to her new contractor.

Chapter Two

Kane let out a long breath, feeling some of the nervous energy leave his body. This was exactly the kind of job he loved—taking something so run-down and bringing it back to its former glory. But Dr. Captain Julia Fitzgerald was exactly the kind of client that he most assuredly did *not* love.

He'd first noticed the blonde woman the second she'd sat down at the counter of the Cowgirl Up Café. It was hard not to notice a pretty face like that, despite the fact that she'd kept mostly to herself and didn't make eye contact with any of the other customers.

Not that he'd been in a real friendly mood himself these past two years. But before he knew it, the woman had her arms wrapped around him, her small, firm breasts pressed up against his back, and suddenly he hadn't cared about the vegetables he'd accidentally bitten into because all he could think about was his desire for her clasped hands to travel downward. He'd reacted so quickly, almost knocking his head into her face, that he wasn't quite sure what they'd even talked about after that. He'd seen a flush of embarrassment steal up her cheeks, and she'd pointed at something in his teeth before the entire restaurant broke out into laughter. Then she was gone before he could find out who she was.

An hour later, he still hadn't recovered from the unexpected shock of seeing the same woman standing next to Freckles on the front porch. Nor had he stopped anxiously wiping his mouth or checking his teeth for residual spinach every time he'd passed his reflection in a window. So maybe he'd put on his game face when he'd been formally introduced to her, but she hadn't exactly been real comfortable in his presence, either.

"You sure she's your niece?" Kane asked Freckles now, looking out the kitchen window at Dr. Smarty-Pants sitting in her car, frowning at her cell phone. Yeah, he got the message loud and clear. The young woman was a doctor. She saved lives for a living. Apparently she even tried to save lives during her breakfast. He didn't need a college degree to see that no matter how beautiful she was, she thought she was way too good for the likes of him.

"What? You don't see the family resemblance?" the café-owner-and-sometimes-waitress asked.

He glanced back at the seventy-something-year-old woman, noting that her purple eye shadow was an exact match to the geometric pattern on the scarf tying up her orangeish hair. Just Julia, on the other hand, didn't wear a lick of makeup, and her only accessory had been an ugly beige cardigan covering up the hospital scrubs he hadn't noticed earlier at the café.

"Well, she's almost as pretty as you, but she kind of reminds me of one of those Lego people I had when I was a boy," he said, then tried to offer the woman his most charming smile. His mouth and his opinions had often gotten him into trouble before, and he hoped Freckles didn't object to his honesty.

But the sassy older lady just beamed a crooked grin, then sauntered over to join him by the window. "Yeah, she's a little stiff and formal, but she'll come around once I give her a good makeover."

Actually, Kane would've used the words *cold* and *inanimate* to describe her. Just Julia was exactly like those academic decathlon snobs Kane had avoided in high school. The ones who were standoffish and thought less of him because he was some dumb jock. Not counting the high-handed way she'd talked down to him at the café, the woman had barely said three words to him, directing most of her comments to her aunt.

"What's she doing to that poor phone?" he asked when he saw Julia shake the device before throwing it onto the dash of her car and backing out of the driveway.

Freckles sighed. "Poor girl's not so good with technology. But don't you dare tell her I said that. She's used to being the best at whatever she sets her mind to."

"I'll bet that doesn't help much when it comes to interpersonal relationships," he said.

"You're one to talk, Kane Chatterson," Freckles responded, and he could see the disapproval in every wrinkle on her face. A wave of remorse lodged in his gut. As usual, he'd said the first thing that popped into his mind, not thinking that it might come out as an insult. He was always too quick, too impulsive. "We all have our flaws, son."

Kane didn't want to think about the reasons that he'd practically been hiding out in Sugar Falls for the past few months. So he wiggled his eyebrows and shot a grin at Freckles instead. "And what exactly are *your* flaws?"

"None of your beeswax, you little charmer." She smacked his arm lightly, and the playful gesture helped loosen the knot in his gut. "And speaking of charm, don't you get any ideas about putting those famous Chatterson moves on my Julia, you hear?"

"Ha!" Kane tried to laugh. "What famous moves?"

"She's not real savvy when it comes to people, especially anything involving business and dating. She's too trusting. She needs worldly people like us to look out for her."

"I think you're doing a fine job of looking out for her." *All on your own*, he thought, but didn't dare say out loud. In fact, Kane pitied the man who was stupid enough to get on Freckles's bad side. And not just because they'd be banned from her restaurant and the best chicken-fried steak in Idaho.

"You keep that in mind. Julia's nothing like those major-league groupies you got used to when you were playing baseball."

He tried not to roll his eyes. How could he get anything from his notorious past out of his mind when everywhere he turned, it was getting brought up? Most people in town knew not to bring up his past career as a major-league pitcher or the scandal in Chicago if they wanted to engage Kane in more than five minutes of conversation. And usually five minutes was his max. Which meant this little chat with Freckles had gone on way too long.

"Don't worry. I'll give your niece a fair price, and you can rest assured that I have absolutely no intention of bringing the so-called Chatterson moves out of retirement." He pulled the antique watch out of the pocket of his jeans and clicked the cover open and closed a few times. "Come on. I'll give you a ride back to the café so you can make me a new burrito."

"Fine, but you're paying full price for a second meal." Freckles sighed and hopped up into the Bronco. She was much sprier than most women her age—whatever age that was. "So, you're saying my niece isn't attractive or smart enough for you?"

"That's not what I said at all, and you know it." He slammed the door a little more forcefully than necessary, wanting to cut off any further discussion on this subject. People with half their eyesight could see that Just Julia was drop-dead gorgeous, even if she kept her classic beauty hidden underneath those ugly hospital clothes and an aloof exterior. He wasn't about to admit to Freckles— or anyone—that every muscle in his body hardened the moment she'd reached out and shaken his hand. Kane hadn't been remodeling homes for long, but he already had a few rules for himself.

Rule Number One. He worked alone.

Rule Number Two. He always packed an extra sandwich in case time got away from him and he found himself on the job after dinnertime, which happened nearly every day.

Rule Number Three. He wouldn't work for a client who didn't have the same vision he did for the outcome of the property. Some people might think this was bad business sense, but it wasn't as though Kane was in this line of work for the money. He didn't believe in working for free, but his past salary and careful investing pretty much negated the need for him ever to work again. He'd started this business because he loved to build things and see his ideas come to life, not because he loved being around people.

Today, he would add Rule Number Four. He wouldn't

date a client, no matter how attracted he was to her. That would be an easy enough rule to follow. Unlike Just Julia, Kane's heart wasn't in need of protection. It was retired, along with his pitching glove.

"So, what do you see for the house?" Kane asked her aunt as he climbed in and started up the classic car he'd been refurbishing in his spare time.

He listened to Freckles's chatter as he steered the Bronco back into town, noting that all of her suggestions were the complete opposite of what her niece wanted. Which, actually, made following Rule Number Three rather easy. He and Just Julia definitely saw eye to eye about keeping the same features of the stately old house and just repairing and refinishing everything to bring it back to its original splendor.

Kane turned onto Snowflake Boulevard, the street that ran through downtown Sugar Falls, and pulled in front of the Cowgirl Up Café to let Freckles out. Neither his stomach nor his still-tense muscles were settled yet and he promised her he would stop in for lunch instead. He waved to a few of the locals, keeping his green cap pulled down low just in case there were any tourists out and about looking for an autograph or a sly selfie with the elusive "Legend" Chatterson.

God, he hated that nickname. And he'd grown to hate the celebrity status that came along with it.

What he *did* like was the slower pace of the small town, along with the refuge and the anonymity it had provided him. So far. The scandal of Brawlgate was finally dying down, and he didn't want to challenge fate by coming out of hiding too soon. Plus, Kane was finding that as much as he missed pitching, there was something to be said for living out of the spotlight. Despite fielding the occasional calls from his sports agent and former coaches, he was free to do whatever he wanted. Like tinker on his old cars and rebuild homes. And right now, there was a deteriorating Victorian on Pinecone Court calling his name.

As he drove back to the house, he reached under his seat and pulled out a notepad. So maybe he hadn't been completely honest about not needing that. Kane parked the car and grabbed a tape measure from his tool bag in the backseat. Because he had issues focusing, Kane had a tendency to get so absorbed in a project that he would forget about his surroundings and tune out everything and everyone around him. And when that happened, he preferred not to have potential clients think he was off his rocker.

Since he hadn't given the key back to Freckles yet, he could spend some more time in the house on his own, exploring it and making notes.

He just hoped that when he made those notes and calculated the costs, he didn't spell anything wrong or add incorrectly on the formal estimate.

Concentrating on schoolwork had never been his strong suit, and he'd rather have a busload of newscasters from ESPN roll into Sugar Falls and reveal his hiding spot than have Just Julia look down her cute, smarty-pants nose at him.

By the time he pulled into a visitor parking spot at Shadowview Military Hospital the second Thursday in November, Kane was already five minutes late for his group session. Well, not *his* group session—one run by his brother-in-law, Drew.

He stopped by the Starbucks kiosk in the lobby and ordered a decaf Frappuccino because he hated sitting still in those introductory meetings with nothing to do, nothing to hold on to. Unable to wait, he stuck his tongue through the hole of the domed plastic lid to taste the whipped cream, then kept his head down as he walked through the large, plain lobby. Kane navigated his way down the fall-themed decorated corridors of the first floor until he found the psychology department, which was directly across from the physical rehab department.

Dr. Drew Gregson had explained that he wanted his patients with PTSD to understand their therapy was no different than someone learning how to walk again after losing a limb. Tonight he was meeting with a new group in a classroom-like setting—and Kane hated classrooms. They would eventually meet out on the track, in the weight room and on various courts and fields.

When Kane had been doing physical therapy after his shoulder surgery, his sister, Kylie, had talked him into coming to work out at the hospital. Drew had been looking for innovative ways to assist his PTSD patients in their recovery, and helped his wife convince Kane that exercising with them would be a great motivator for some of the men and women who used athletics as a physical outlet. Especially since most of the group's sessions ended up in some challenge that usually provided one of the patients with bragging rights that they'd competed against Legend Chatterson.

Good thing his ego could take it. Being at Shadow-view—seeing the world through the eyes of the wounded warriors and the staff who helped them—always put things into perspective for Kane. These people were dealing with legitimate life-or-death situations. Brawlgate, his former baseball career, being attracted to his new client...none of that seemed as important when he was faced with real obstacles to overcome.

Kane looked at the number he'd written on his hand

to make sure he was going to the right meeting room. Which was why he didn't see the shapely blonde exiting the gym facilities until she'd bumped into him.

"Sorry, darlin'," he said before thinking about it. The flirtatious endearment sounded as out of practice as his pitching arm. His first instinct was to pull an orange pumpkin-shaped piece of construction paper off the nearby bulletin board and hide his face behind it, but then he recognized those round green eyes.

Whoa. His hand flew to his mouth to make sure he didn't have any whipped cream stuck to his face. He hadn't seen her since she'd signed off on his estimate and he'd started work on her old house a few days after they first met. Neither time had she looked so flushed, and sexy, and...hell, feminine, as she did now.

Not that he wasn't well aware of how attractive she was. But Just Julia in her boxy hospital scrubs only served as a reminder that she was some smart doctor with a fancy education. In this outfit—he let his eyes travel down her form-fitting workout clothes—she looked like the kind of woman who would hang out in hotel bars and throw herself at the visiting professional baseball team.

"Mr. Chatterson?" she asked, and Kane tried not to look at the straps of her sports bra as he shifted the cold drink to his other hand, then back again.

"Sorry. I didn't recognize you dressed like..." Dressed like what? One of Beyoncé's backup dancers? Nothing he could say at this point would make him sound like less of an infatuated idiot. "Anyway, I wasn't expecting to run into you here."

"Sorry for running into you at all," she said, then held up her smartphone. "I wasn't paying attention to where I was going because I have this new fitness monitor on here, and I somehow programmed it wrong. It's telling me that I've only burned thirty calories but that my heart rate is 543. Now, I'm trying to just delete the whole thing, because really, I know how to check my own pulse and multiply and... Sorry. You probably don't want to hear about this."

She tapped harder on the display. Kane, always a sucker for video games and electronics, eased the phone out of her hand. "Here, let me."

She leaned in and watched over his shoulder as he made a few swipes and closed out the app. He didn't have the heart to tell her that touch screens didn't seem to be her forte. Or that standing this close to her still-damp skin made him think of a different type of physical exertion he wouldn't mind engaging in with her.

He finished and handed the device back to her, cursing to himself for having such an inappropriate thought. "What are you doing here, anyway?"

"Well, I *do* work here." It might've come off as defensive or stuck-up from any other woman, but Just Julia's response seemed more like a schoolteacher trying to explain a new concept to a first grader.

And Kane Chatterson had always had a soft spot for his first-grade teacher, who'd been the only one who hadn't treated him like a below-average student with problems sitting still in class.

"Are you working now?" He finally allowed himself to look down at the form-fitting sports tank that tapered down to her small waist. He brought his straw to his lips, needing something to relieve the sudden dryness in his mouth. He got the paper wrapper instead.

"I had back-to-back surgeries this morning and needed to loosen up and relieve some tension before I started on my post-op reports. Normally I do laps in the pool, but there was a water aerobics class going on, so I used the cardio equipment instead and accidentally set the program for the inverted pyramid. The incline level got stuck on high, which is why I tried to use my phone to calculate my heart rate. Wait. Why am I explaining all this to you?"

"Because I have the kind of face that makes people want to open up?" Why was he being so damn flirty? It was as if he couldn't stop the asinine comments from flying out. But she'd caught him off guard, looking like that. Plus, she was much more down-to-earth and endearing when she rambled on about nothing.

"Your face is perfect. It's your eyes that make people feel as if they're strapped to a polygraph machine." That was an interesting revelation. Did he make her nervous?

"So you like my face?" He reached up to stroke his trademark beard, then remembered he'd shaved it several months ago when he'd moved to Sugar Falls. Instead he touched a bristly jawline that felt like eighty-grit sandpaper.

"I'm not going to answer that." But he could tell by the blush rising up from her neckline that she probably liked his appearance more than she wanted to admit. An alarm bell went off inside his brain. And then, as if she'd heard the same warning, she straightened her back and crossed her arms, her haughty stance effectively putting him back in his place. "What are *you* doing here?"

"I'm here for the…" He stopped. Kane couldn't very well tell her he came as a guest to help boost troop morale. That might give away his celebrity status.

"I'm here for a meeting," Kane finally said, then shifted his drink in his hands again and prayed she wouldn't look at the big Psychology Department sign behind him.

She looked, and he saw her green eyes become round with realization.

"Therapy is nothing to be ashamed of," she said, surprising him. No, he didn't suppose it was, for a brain doctor like her. The only thing he was embarrassed of was the fact that he'd called this uptight, intelligent woman *darlin'* and that she might connect the dots and figure out who he really was. Assuming she hadn't already.

"Oh really?" He seized on her mistake. "Do you go?"

"As a matter of fact, Aunt Freckles suggested I start talking to a professional about my... Well, that's not really relevant."

Oh boy. The smart doctor had a secret. Besides the fact that she'd been hiding all her sexy curves under those blue scrubs and ugly cardigan sweaters. Now Kane was more than curious about what else the doctor was keeping under wraps.

"Actually..." She shifted back on her sneakers and stood up straighter. "I've been meaning to call you and see how the progress is going on the upstairs bedrooms."

Bedrooms. Bedrooms. He tried not to think about the fact that this Lycra-clad woman had just said the word *bedrooms* to him. "Progress? Well, the flooring is all done in two of them and down most of the hallway. I should have the stairway finished by next Wednesday. I'm still waiting for you to get back to me on those tile samples so I can start the master bathroom. Why?"

"I was just thinking that with the colder weather approaching, I'd like to move in soon so I can appease my aunt. She's worried that since I'm living close to work, I don't have much of a social life and... Sorry. I'm rambling again."

"You mean you want to move into the place while it's still under construction?"

"I promise I wouldn't be in your way or anything. I'm

usually at the hospital all day and would keep to one bedroom and bathroom upstairs."

"Stop saying *bedroom*," he muttered.

"What was that?"

"I said 'spraying bedroom.' As in, I need to use my paint gun to finish spraying the last coat on it. The bathroom will still take at least a week once I order those tiles. But I haven't even started on the kitchen yet, and your aunt was pretty convinced that you needed a fully functional kitchen before you could move in."

Julia sighed. "Aunt Freckles is convinced about a lot of things that I don't actually need. You should see the liquid eyeliner she bought me so I could practice something called the cat-wing technique." Kane didn't reply that Just Julia's aunt was probably right about the kitchen and most definitely wrong about the eyeliner. Or the fact that he preferred working on empty houses where the pretty and distracting homeowners weren't coming and going anytime they pleased. Especially if this was her normal after-work attire. "Anyway, I'll head back to my office now to look over those tile samples, and then we'll plan on me moving into the house next week."

She didn't wait for his response as she nodded at him, then walked away. Her expensive-looking sneakers squeaked along the pristine hospital floor with each step. He had a feeling brain surgeons—not to mention military officers—were used to telling people what to do and having their orders carried out.

Apparently the boss lady didn't understand that Kane Chatterson wasn't a lower ranked recruit or some unemployed laborer in a small hick town perfectly content to do her bidding. He might not have a bunch of letters after his name, but he had two championship rings and had been on the cover of *Sports Illustrated* three times. Even if one of those times was a shot taken during Brawlgate and wasn't the most flattering image.

No wonder she didn't have much of a social life, if this was how she talked to people. He definitely wasn't some nobody to be so easily dismissed. And if the good doctor thought she was going to move in and start ordering him around as he remodeled her home, she'd better think again.

Chapter Three

Julia hadn't minded when Freckles had hired a personal shopper who emailed links containing possible dresses for Julia to wear to the hospital's fund-raising gala in December. After all, shopping was an easy enough task to delegate since Julia didn't exactly care what she wore to the event, which was still four weeks away. The thing she wasn't looking forward to, though, was finding a suitable date to accompany her, which Aunt Freckles insisted was just as necessary as a new pair of strappy heels.

Julia sat at her desk, looking at the dark screen of her cell phone, and groaned when she was unable to open the message her aunt had sent when she'd been downstairs working out. Then she squeezed her eyes shut and sent out a prayer that Kane Chatterson hadn't seen the embarrassing text when he'd helped her reprogram her phone twenty minutes ago.

Heat stole up her cheeks as she squeezed her eyes

shut and gave her ponytail a firm shake. Julia refused to think about how her contractor had stared at her when she ran into him outside the gym. Especially since she had many more pressing matters to worry about—like how to make Aunt Freckles proud of her without allowing the woman full access to her sparse wardrobe and even sparser dating options.

Setting boundaries was usually easy for Julia because she didn't tend to socialize much anyway. But this was uncharted territory for her. How did Julia politely tell her well-meaning relative that she absolutely did not need a makeover or a professional relationship coach—as the last text suggested?

Surely it couldn't be that difficult to find her own date. All she needed to do was figure out what kind of man she wanted and then go out and find one. She shoved a few chocolate-covered raisins in her mouth as she wrote "Qualities I Want in a Man" at the top of a notepad.

But the only image that came to her mind was Kane Chatterson standing there, all perceptive and broad-shouldered and rugged. Sure, Julia had come into contact with plenty of men since joining the Navy, but dress whites and blue utilities were utterly dull compared to the faded jeans and soft flannel uniform her hired contractor filled out. The man was broad, but lean and muscular in that athletic way of someone who was always on the move. He was also more intense than a college freshman studying for his first midterm, looking around as if he was taking in every detail of his surroundings and then memorizing it for future use.

Besides the condescending smirk, she'd only seen Kane wearing a constant frown, barely addressing her unless it was to ask about paint colors or refinished hardwood floors. So she'd been shocked an hour ago when she'd heard the man call her *darlin'* in that slow, sexy drawl of his. Shocked and then flushed with embarrassment when she realized he'd been staring at her body as though he'd spilled some of his iced coffee drink on her and wanted to lick it off.

Then she'd said something about therapy and the guy's whole demeanor had changed. Julia had tried to come up with something else to talk about, but she'd just ended up blabbering about bedrooms and moving in and eyeliners, then tried to walk away with her head held as high as the uncomfortable, tingling tightness in her neck had allowed.

Stop. Stop thinking about what happened in the hospital corridor earlier. No wonder her aunt didn't believe she was capable of finding a suitable date on her own.

This was ridiculous. She could do this. Julia had never failed at a task, and she wasn't about to get distracted and fail now.

She looked down at the empty page and began to write.

Must look good in flannel.

Must speak in a slow, sexy drawl.

Must look at me like I'm the whipped cream on his Frappuccino.

No, *this* was ridiculous. She tore the yellow sheet off and tossed it in the small trash can by her desk.

She rotated the pencil between her fingers, twirling it like a miniature baton. After a disastrous relationship with one of her professors a few years ago, Julia didn't want a man at all, let alone another person to help her find one. She knew that her solitary upbringing and current avoidance of social activities was anything but ordinary. She'd never let it bother her before now. But her fitting in seemed important to Aunt Freckles. And if she wanted to be normal, or at least create the appearance of being normal on the night of the hospital gala, then she would need to put forth more effort. She looked down at a fresh piece of paper and started her list all over again, this time leaving off any references to Kane Chatterson.

She had just finished and put her pencil down when a knock sounded at her office door. Chief Wilcox, Julia's surgical assistant, entered. "Do you have those post-op reports done? The physical therapist is already asking for them."

"Yes, they should be in the patient's online file," Julia told the corpsman, who had a pink backpack slung over her shoulder and was apparently leaving for the day.

"I looked there and didn't see them."

"I finished them after my workout," Julia said, pulling up the screen on her iPad. "Oh. I must not have clicked on Submit. Okay, they should be in there now. I'll call the physical therapist and let him know." She looked her assistant over. "You look like you're off for the weekend."

Even to Julia, the observation came out sounding a little too obvious. She didn't want the woman to think she was crossing the line from professional to overly social, but how else was she supposed to get to know her staff? She told herself this was good practice.

"Oh, yeah. A few of us are doing a camping trip up near the Sugar River trailhead. I still need to pack my gear, and Chief Filbert put me in charge of KP duty, so I need to get all the food ready, too."

Julia had no idea who Filbert was, but she was more than familiar with the hollowness circling her chest. Not that she was much of a camper, but it was her weekend off, as well, and nobody had thought to ask if she'd like to go on the trip. Same thing with happy hours or lunches in the break room. It was easier to act indifferent than to make other people see that she, too, wanted to be included in the ordinary adventures of life.

At a loss, Julia simply said, "I hope you all enjoy your trip, then. I'll see you back here on Monday at 0600."

"Aye, aye, Cap'," Wilcox said before closing the door. Julia fell back against her chair and squeezed her eyes shut at how ridiculously pathetic she must've sounded. She remembered her first day of high school and how the students patted her on her twelve-year-old head when she'd foolishly asked several of the cheerleaders if she could sit with them at their table. Nobody had been rude to her outright, but the novelty of having a child genius as some sort of odd little mascot soon wore off when Julia easily outscored several of the seniors on their honors English midterms.

College hadn't been any better, especially since she was studying adolescent brain development while her own brain hadn't finished the process. Guidance counselors who didn't know what to do with such a young scholar told her things would get better for her socially once she got older. But by the time she started med school, she no longer cared about what others thought of her and found it easier to simply hang back and observe. She had her cello, she had swimming, she had her books and her studies. She didn't have time for homecoming games and celebratory drinks after final exams—even if she *had* been old enough to be admitted into the bars with the rest of her classmates.

A career in research had been on the horizon until she'd seen a documentary about women in the military. She'd attended Officer Development School soon after her parents died, the order and regulation of the Navy reminding her of her regimented childhood and serving as the perfect antidote to Julia's hesitancy to fraternize. She easily told herself that she wasn't jealous of her staff's camaraderie or the fact that she looked for reasons to sit here in her office and work instead of going back to the lonely officers' quarters and microwaving a frozen Lean Cuisine before falling asleep on her government-issue twin-size mattress.

So why was she all of a sudden starting to worry about any of it now? She undid her ponytail and massaged her scalp before turning to the tile samples she'd set on the credenza behind her.

Julia ran her fingers over the glazed surfaces of the colorful porcelain pieces. Kane had suggested neutral colors because they added to the resale value. While some of the decorating magazines she'd perused pushed the idea of an all-white bathroom, the surgeon in her worried that she would grow tired of the sterile and clinical feel of such a contrast-free environment.

Julia brought the blue-and-green mosaic strips to her desk and propped them against some medical texts so she could get a better look at them. If they laid the glass tiles in a running bond pattern in the shower, she could use both colors, but would it overpower the white cabinets and the large, claw-foot tub in the center of the room?

She shook some more Raisinets out of the box as she contemplated the color scheme. Not that she was the type who turned to food for comfort—Fitzgeralds didn't need comforting, after all—but during med school, she'd found that she thought better when she snacked.

Unfortunately, no amount of snacking could get Kane's voice out of her mind. She tried to ignore the warmth spreading through her at the memory of her body's response to his assessing stare outside the gym.

The sooner she made a selection, the sooner she could get back to more important things—like picking a dress for the hospital gala and finding an appropriate date to take with her. Preferably one that didn't look at her as though he knew exactly how much she wanted those sexy, smirking lips to …

Julia snatched another handful of candy, determined to distract herself from thinking of his mouth, only to have her focus shift to the blue-green glass tiles that were the exact same shade as his eyes. If she chose that color, would she be sentencing herself to a lifetime of showers feeling as though his penetrating gaze was surrounding her naked body?

She reached for the plain white subway tiles before changing her mind and grabbing her smartphone. After taking a quick picture, she fired off an email to Kane in an effort to prevent herself from wasting any more of her time with such dangerous and unproductive thoughts. And to stop the sound of his slow drawl calling her *darlin'* replaying over and over again in her mind.

It was after eleven o'clock, and Kane's brain had yet to slow down enough to make going to bed an option. Usually a day's physical labor followed by a long, mind-numbing run after dinner was enough to tire him out sufficiently so that it would take only about thirty minutes for him finally to drop off into his standard six hours of sleep. But images of his client in all her spandex workout glory wouldn't stop popping into his overactive mind, and he decided he might as well pull out his laptop and do some invoices in an effort to bore himself to sleep.

He could go out to his garage and work on his Bronco,

but because of his attention issues, once he got hyper-focused on a project, he would lose all sense of time and end up exhausted and cranky the following day.

So, it was either crunching numbers or watching a late-night edition of *SportsCenter*, which he knew from past experience would only get him more frustrated.

Picking the mentally healthier and more productive option, he sat up and switched on his bedside lamp before opening his nearby laptop. He logged onto his email and, in his inbox, he saw the very name of the source of his late-night thoughts. He clicked on the attached image and stared at her tile selection. He had to give credit to Just Julia. She wasn't too outlandish in her remodeling requests. In fact, Kane had originally suggested white just because the doctor seemed like a plain vanilla kind of person. But seeing the bold colors of the tiles she'd picked—as well as the snug fabric of her high-end athletic wear—made him rethink his original opinion. She'd typed information about the brand and tracking numbers in the body of the email. But he squinted at the bottom left of the picture, seeing notes written on a yellow notepad off to the side.

Although today's encounter at the hospital made it a total of three times they'd seen each other in person, he'd emailed her with updates, and she'd stopped by the house in the evenings when he wasn't there and left pictures carefully cut out of magazines along with handwritten descriptions on lined paper taped to the walls. Usually her notes were detailed instructions of what she liked or wanted, and even though they were long and tiresome to read, Kane would much rather deal with a client on paper than one in the flesh.

Especially one whose curvaceous, damp flesh he'd been thinking about all evening.

So when he saw the note by the bluish green tiles, his first instinct was to zoom in and see what special instructions she had for him now. Instead, he leaned closer as he read the words "Qualities I Want in a Man."

What in the world was this? His finger vibrated over the mouse pad, but refused to click on the button that would close the image.

By the time he got to number three, he tried to tell himself that this obviously wasn't meant for him to see. Yet like a pitch in midhurl, he couldn't stop now. Why in the world would she write out such a ridiculous and pointless list? Or one so personal?

Assuming she was the one who'd written it in the first place.

It was her handwriting, though. He'd exchanged plans and inventories with her long enough to know that the woman put a ton of thought into *every* list she created. Freckles had made several offhand remarks this past week regarding her niece's single status and lack of a social life. Maybe Just Julia was feeling inadequate in that department and was making an effort to step up her game.

His eyes bounced around the enlarged image, trying to take all the information in at once while he told himself that there was no way he'd make the cut. Not that he *wanted* her looking in his direction, anyway. Kane had to take a few deep breaths to focus on what he was reading. Hell, were there any qualities on here that he even remotely possessed? He read it through again.

Must be social.

That certainly wasn't him. Sure, it used to be, before his career had taken a nosedive, but nowadays, Kane viewed social situations like most batters viewed a curve-ball—confusing and oftentimes unavoidable.

Must be educated and able to discuss current events.

Nope. Kane Chatterson barely sat still long enough in class to make it out of high school with a diploma. He had a feeling even that accomplishment was the result of sympathetic teachers and his dad's generous donation to the library building fund.

Must be patient and not lose his temper.

Kylie once told him that he had the patience of a hummingbird, which said a lot, considering his sister's only speed was overdrive.

Must enjoy swimming or similar civilized athletic pursuits.

Sure, baseball could be civilized if compared to rugby or ice hockey or cage fighting, for instance. But as any of the three million YouTube viewers would attest, the swinging bats and punches and profanity involved in the Brawlgate scandal two years ago were anything but civil.

Strong.

In terms of what? Before his shoulder injury, Kane could bench-press two-fifty and hurl a fastball ninety-nine miles per hour. But Erica, his ex, had once called him emotionally unavailable and a weak excuse for a boyfriend. So he was fifty-fifty in the strength department.

Good with his hands.

Kane looked at his palms, trying to imagine how his work-worn, callous hands would compare with the uppity doctor's long, graceful fingers that meticulously saved lives. Meh.

Flannel.

He glanced at his open closet and the soft plaid shirts hanging in order by color. He had a feeling the prim Navy captain meant the man she was looking for must prefer wearing flannel pajamas or some other conservative outfit to bed.

Kane stretched out under his quilt and tried not to grin at how shocked Just Julia would be if she could see the complete lack of flannel between his sheets right now. Or the complete lack of any material, for that matter.

The sudden thought of the attractive woman seeing him naked in bed caused an unexpected response, and Kane had to shift his computer lower on his lap.

Speaking of lists, maybe he should rethink the set of rules he'd laid out for himself. Specifically, the one about him not dating his clients. Or thinking about their damp blond hair pulled back away from their high, flushed cheekbones.

Kane shook his head, trying to envision Just Julia in plain blue scrubs and an oversize white coat. If he concentrated hard enough, maybe he could imagine her green eyes looking through him, instead of being dilated from physical exertion and rounded in surprise when she'd glanced up from her cell phone and collided with him in the hospital hallway earlier today.

He slammed the laptop closed in frustration, then remembered their conversation and her plan to move into her house in a week. Kane needed to get as much work as possible done before then so he wouldn't have to risk running into her upstairs. Near her bedroom. He opened the computer again and logged on to the building supply store's website to place an order for the tiles.

That done, he set his laptop off to the side and turned out his lamp, knowing he wouldn't be able to fall asleep for a long time. After a few minutes, he pulled the laptop over again, opened his email account and finally sent her a reply, using as few words as he dared.

Ordered tile. Should be in stock next Wed. Then, at the last second, he couldn't help adding, Kitchen not done. Maybe that would stall her and he could buy himself some more time. And avoid running into the pretty doctor at all costs.

Julia carried the last box down the stairs from her officer's quarters and shoved it into the backseat of her red MINI Cooper. How sad was it that all of her personal belongings fit into a car with the cubic space of a safe-deposit box? Well, technically, the attic at the Georgetown house was filled with family heirlooms and photo albums and her parents' personal effects. Yet none of that had ever really felt like hers.

Still, she would have to face that mess eventually, or have one of her attorneys face it for her and send her an invoice. She looked at her watch and estimated that the sun would set before she made it to Sugar Falls. She'd purposely timed her move-in day to be more of a move-in evening. That way she wouldn't have to see Kane Chatterson and risk him asking her in person if she'd gotten a cookbook like she'd promised her Aunt Freckles.

By the time she pulled onto Pinecone Court thirty

minutes later, her stomach was empty, yet she was eager to see what progress had been made on her house. When she saw the Ford Bronco parked along her curb, now sporting a dull gray paint color instead of its usual rust spots, she wanted to throw her gearshift straight into Reverse.

Instead she took a deep breath and ordered her tummy to quit thrashing around. She would really need to become accustomed to seeing Kane sporadically. After all, she'd hired the guy to remodel her house. She couldn't very well let her abdominal muscles get all tight and contracted anytime she saw his ugly old car.

She wasn't some lovesick nineteen-year-old anymore, thinking an affair with her college professor was the real deal. In fact, technically speaking, *she* was *Kane's* boss. She was a Navy officer, trained to issue orders. And she was an accomplished surgeon, known for her steady hand and her even steadier nerves. If she could command an operating room full of experienced hospital staff, Julia could certainly handle one small-town contractor who barely said more than a few words to her—even if his eyes drank her in as though they knew every inch of her body intimately.

She parked in the narrow driveway, then grabbed her leather satchel and one of the boxes out of the backseat and made her way up to the front porch and inside. She heard music coming from upstairs and smelled something garlicky drifting out of the kitchen area. She set the box down in the front parlor and climbed the newly finished stairway, uncertain if she should be walking on the freshly stained steps. But then she realized they must be dry, since someone was upstairs and had to have walked on them already.

She followed the sound of Duke Ellington—her classical cello instructor would've frowned at her recognizing the piece—toward her bedroom and stepped into the well-lit area, relieved that the antique chandelier had been installed already. When she got to the bathroom door, she froze. Kane Chatterson, wearing faded jeans and nothing but paint splatters on his torso, was standing behind her claw-foot tub, one well-defined muscular arm poised with a paintbrush above the top sill of the window frame.

With an effort, she ignored the weakness in her legs and drew in one ragged breath after another.

Each stroke of his hand matched the swaying tempo of the music coming from the cordless speaker propped up on the bathroom vanity. The muscles of his back moved in an orchestrated rhythm with the jazzy strains of a piano. The darkness outside made his reflection in the window almost mirror-like, and she saw the deep-set focus in his eyes, his concentrated brow and the hard lines of his set jaw. She could also see that he was completely transfixed in his own little world and had no idea she was there.

The professional in her wanted to cough or turn down the jazz music or do something to draw his attention to the fact that he wasn't alone. Unfortunately, her body wasn't behaving so professionally. Desire curled around her, squeezing so tightly it threatened to cut off the oxygen supply to her brain. Thank God the man was focused too intensely to witness her intrusion on his workspace because Julia didn't think she could've taken a step.

She had no idea how long she stood there, just as absorbed in his movements as he apparently was in his painting. A softer, slower saxophone-based song switched on the moment his eyes met hers, and Julia wasn't sure if the dizziness in her head was from the paint fumes or from the way he looked at her.

Chapter Four

Kane was so engrossed in what he was doing, he had no idea how long Julia had been standing there waiting for him. He struggled to get those old feelings of embarrassment in check before turning away from the window and pretending not to care that she'd caught him completely off guard. Noting her surgical scrubs were covered by a soft purple cardigan sweater, he let out a breath, equally relieved and disappointed that she wasn't wearing her exercise outfit.

"Hey," he said, before coughing and clearing his throat. He set the paintbrush down in the tray and walked over to his iPhone to turn off his playlist. "I wasn't expecting you so soon."

"It's seven o'clock," she said, her green eyes round and fringed with spiky lashes.

Kane pulled his late Grandpa Chatterson's antique gold watch out of his pocket and snapped it open—more as something to redirect his focus than to actually check the time. "Wow. I must've really been in the zone."

At least, that's what his dad called it whenever Kane would tune out the rest of the world to the point that someone could ask him if he wanted a million dollars and he'd ignore the question. His mom called it hyper-focusing. He called it a pain-in-the-butt symptom of his ADHD.

"I, uh, didn't mean to startle you," she said, but he noticed she wasn't looking at him when she spoke. Correction: she was definitely looking at him, just not at his face. The skin across his bare chest tightened, causing his pectoral muscles to flex slightly. He remembered her list and wanted to suggest she add something about physical attraction as a quality she might appreciate in a man. Not that he considered himself all that attractive, but after several years of playing professional sports and living out of hotels, plagued by groupies and jersey chasers, he knew when a lady was sizing him up. Or at least when he *hoped* she was.

"That's a decently sized incision, there," she said. Not cut. Not wound. *Incision.* So maybe the doctor wasn't sizing him up so much as taking a professional interest in his anatomy. An unexpected feeling of disappointment washed down his torso. "When did you have a full shoulder replacement?" she asked.

He squinted at his shoulder before looking at her doubtfully. Maybe she *did* know who he was after all. She'd have to be living under a rock to not know, but the few times he'd met Just Julia, he'd gotten the impression that was where she liked to keep herself hidden. "So you heard about my surgery?"

"No. I can tell from your incision."

Of course she could. Otherwise she wouldn't have asked when he'd had it. Rather than making himself look like more of an idiot, he tried to concentrate on her words as she kept talking. "Your surgeon used the extended deltopectoral approach, which is normally only suitable for total shoulder replacement with an open reduction and internal fixation of a proximal humeral fracture."

He ran his hand across the lower half of his face, but that didn't make him resent her easy use of fancy medical jargon any less. "You sure like to use a lot of big words, doc."

"Here," she said, walking toward him. He tried not to flinch when she traced her finger along the pink scar tissue. "Your incision extends from the outer end of your clavicle to the coracoid and follows the medial edge of the deltoid muscle."

She must've mistaken his annoyance for a lack of understanding since she was now restating the obvious as though he hadn't been the one to undergo the procedure. However, he couldn't be sure since he could barely hear her voice over his own heartbeat pounding in his ears. The soft caress of her cool finger was making gooseflesh rise on his exposed skin.

"Why would someone your age need such an extensive surgery?" she asked, and he could feel the warmth of her breath.

Would she believe him if he said "car accident"? Probably not. Dr. Smarty-Pants was proving to be too damn intelligent for Kane's own good. But right this second, with her finger still tracing his scar and sending shockwaves throughout his body, he really didn't want to think about the pissed off player who'd charged the mound and attacked him with a Louisville Slugger. "Random baseball bat injury."

"Hmm." His eyes were drawn to her mouth. She didn't wear an ounce of makeup, not even lipstick, but the pink fullness of her upper lip was enhanced by the deep bow in the center. "That must have been quite a baseball bat. Still…"

When she shook her head, Kane caught a whiff of her shampoo, and he was reminded of the coconut and mango smoothies he'd loved as a child when his family used to vacation in Hawaii. He leaned in, his face hovering closer to hers. "Still, what?"

"It's just that even blunt force trauma from a bat wouldn't necessitate a full shoulder replacement. Usually a humerus fracture is associated with pathological fractures and osteoporosis. You must've been diagnosed with early-onset osteoporosis."

It was as if she'd dumped a bucket of cold Gatorade over his head. He immediately took a step back, already regretting how close he'd let her get. Of course his shoulder had already suffered extensive damage just from the long-term wear and tear he'd put on it as a professional pitcher, but he hadn't been willing to listen to the professionals. He had no one to blame for that but himself. Arturo Dominguez and his temper were the icing on Kane's arthritic cake.

"I guess so," he said and pivoted on his booted heel. Not wanting to talk about his career-ending injury or the preexisting condition trainers had warned him about, and definitely not wanting to breathe in the heady fragrance of her tidy blond ponytail, Kane walked over to the corner where he'd left his tool bag and pulled on his discarded T-shirt. "I was just finishing up with the bathroom so it would be all set for you to move in. As you can see, the rest of the house is still a work in progress."

He grabbed the tray of paint and almost slammed his finger shut in the ladder before hauling it out of the room, bumping it on the banister as he hurried out. He didn't have to turn around to know that she was following him downstairs, to a less intimate part of the house. Thankfully.

"The master bedroom and bath are perfect," she said, and he tried not to let the compliment go to his overthinking head. "They're way better than I could've hoped for. You even got the stairs done, so I won't have to worry about my clogs falling through any of that rotted wood."

He looked back at her purple shoes, thinking those things needed more than a hole in the floorboards to cover up their ugliness. Instead, he asked, "Do you need some help carrying your stuff inside?"

"No, that's okay. I only have a couple more boxes in my car. Besides, I saw the pizza sitting on that table thingy in the kitchen and I wouldn't want to keep you from your dinner."

"Actually, that's *your* dinner," he said, following her gaze toward the plywood-covered sawhorses and the white cardboard box with the name Patrelli's stamped on top. "Your aunt picked it up from the Italian restaurant in town and dropped it by here a while ago. She said to keep it warm in the oven for you, but as you can see, no oven yet."

Julia didn't respond and he hoped she was rethinking this whole move-in-while-he-was-still-working-here idea. Not that she needed an oven to heat things up in here. Kane doubted his body could take any more intense encounters like the one in the master bathroom a couple of minutes ago. Her face had been inches from his, her mouth way too close for comfort. His blood was still on fire from the way she'd been staring at him.

Leave, Chatterson, he thought. *Get out before you do something else you'll regret.* He dropped off his supplies in the mudroom and, on his way back through the kitchen, gestured toward the custom-ordered cabinets wedged together under a few drop cloths. "I planned to start installing the cupboards tomorrow, but you'll still need to pick out the appliances before it'll be up to Freckles's standards."

She squished up her nose, making the bow shape of her upper lip more pronounced. "I've been putting that off because I'm really not much of a cook. Yet. But I guess a refrigerator would come in handy."

Was it cockiness that made her think she could master cooking just as easily as she mastered his orthopedic diagnosis? Playing baseball professionally, he'd encountered his fair share of arrogance, and something about Just Julia's demeanor didn't give him that impression about her. Still, her aunt had suggested Dr. Smarty-Pants wasn't used to failing at anything, and because Kane knew firsthand what it was like to fall from grace, he didn't say anything else on the subject.

He walked over to the small cooler he kept near the pantry. "Can I offer you some water or a Gatorade?"

It sounded odd for him to be offering the woman anything in her own home. But judging by her man list, she probably wasn't used to entertaining male guests. Yet. No doubt that was simply another task Just Julia would attempt to master.

The thought of her bringing a guy here made his fingers squeeze the extended water bottle so tightly, the sealed lid threatened to pop off.

"No, thank you. I have a bag of drinks in my car." Then, as if a lightbulb had popped on in her head, she asked, "Would you like some of this pizza? I won't be able to eat it all."

His stomach answered with a small rumble, and Kane realized he hadn't had anything to eat since before noon.

Another side effect of his attention deficit disorder—forgetting to stop and take breaks usually caused his body to punish him later.

Plus, he had a sneaking suspicion, probably fueled by Freckles's pointed comments, that Julia might be a little lonely. Not that he'd expected a moving truck and a parade, but it seemed kind of sad that on a Friday night, nobody was here to help her move into her new place. "Sure. Why don't I help you get the rest of your stuff out of your car, and we can eat after we unload."

"I'd appreciate that. Thanks."

It was asinine to stay another minute under the same roof as the woman, let alone share a meal with her. But if Julia was determined to live here during the remodel, then Kane would have to get used to seeing her and not acting upon this impulse to pull her into his arms and show her exactly what her presence did to his self-control.

He followed her outside and almost tripped on a cardboard box partially hidden by the overgrown grass. "Damn, it's the showerhead I ordered for the master bath. I was going to install it this afternoon, but I must not have heard FedEx delivering it."

Julia shrugged. "Don't worry about it. At least the tub is working. I was actually looking forward to taking a long, hot bath tonight, anyway."

And with that seemingly innocent statement, Kane was again brought back to that moment in her bathroom a few minutes ago when he'd caught her reflection in the window above the tub. His body hardened before he could command his brain to relax. He had absolutely no business imagining Just Julia stripped down naked, submerged under a cluster of bubbles. He had no business imagining her in any way at all.

"Here," she said, handing him a small grocery bag. "This should be light enough for you to handle."

He immediately felt the sting to his pride. "I can carry more than this."

"But what about your shoulder?"

"My shoulder's never been better." To prove his point, he grabbed another box and a bag of what he assumed was more hospital scrubs. "Where's the rest of your stuff? Is it coming later?"

"This is it." She loosely waved at the already half-empty car.

Was she serious? Most of the women he'd dated, including Erica, would pack twice this much for a week's vacation.

"What about furniture?" he asked, trying to balance the load in his arms as he walked up the porch steps.

She shrugged. "I'll have to buy some, I suppose."

"Wait. You don't have a bed. Where will you sleep tonight?"

"I'm going to have a campout."

"A what?"

"A campout." Her excited smile nearly blinded him. "I always wanted to have one when I was younger—you know, with blankets and pillows, building forts in the living room—but my parents didn't like the idea of me messing up the house. I decided that there's no better way to start my new life in my new home than by declaring my own set of rules."

Boy, her parents sounded like a pair of buzzkills. No wonder Dr. Smarty-Pants was so formal and stiff. Growing up in the Chatterson house meant sheets, quilts and toys scattered all over the floor. Having four siblings was fun and kept things interesting, but it was certainly chaotic and… Wait. A basset hound had just lumbered up her driveway and through the side yard. Had she bought a dog, too?

He turned to ask her if they allowed pets in the officer's quarters near Shadowview, but his bad shoulder bumped into the front door frame and he let out a strong curse instead, dropping the armload of stuff he'd bragged would be easy to carry.

"Are you all right?" she asked, those big green eyes looking scandalized by his choice of words.

"Yep. Just wasn't watching where I was going."

"Let me take a look." She set her box on the floor, and he had to hold out his hand to stop her from coming closer.

"No, really. It's fine." The last thing he needed was the sweet doctor touching his body again—even if it was clothed this time. "I've always been a little accident-prone, so I'm used to a few bumps and bruises. How about some pizza?"

Julia looked doubtful, but Kane rolled his shoulder and held back a grimace at the stab of hot pain. "See? It's fine. No big deal."

He walked to the makeshift table and opened the white cardboard box, his lips curling down at the contents. "Uh-oh. We're oh and two with restaurant orders. Looks like Patrelli's forgot the meat."

Her blond ponytail shook back and forth. "No, they didn't. I'm a vegetarian."

Kane couldn't stop the involuntary shudder. "Does your Aunt Freckles know?"

"Yes. She's not too happy about it, either, and says I'll outgrow it by the time I'm in my thirties."

Kane was looking so intently at the pizza, he almost didn't catch her admission. "Your thirties? How old *are* you?"

"Twenty-nine." Her shoulders elevated several inches with the straightening of her spine, and he suspected he'd just hit a nerve. But he didn't care. The math wasn't adding up, and he hated it when problems didn't add up.

"But I thought you were surgeon. Doesn't medical school and all that take a long time?"

"The average is four years for medical school, and depending on your specialty, the neurosurgery residency is another six or seven years."

"But that would be impossible," he said, then saw her eyes turn a darker shade of green, reminding him of that superhero cartoon he used to watch as a kid—the Hulk, where the good guy would get angry and turn green all over.

Not wanting to rile her past the point of no return, he tried to get his brain to calculate the numbers. But she beat him to the punch. "I graduated from high school when I was fourteen. I had a bachelor's in science by age seventeen. I finished med school early, and did my residency right after being commissioned an officer."

He kept staring at her, this obvious genius who truly was a Dr. Smarty-Pants. By the time she was in her mid-teens, she'd already far surpassed the level of education he had now. That familiar baseball-size knot of shame grew to the size of a basketball, and again he wanted to change the subject as soon as possible.

"Why do you always touch your mouth and chin like that?" she asked. He'd been unaware he was doing it, and he shoved his hands in his pockets. "Is it a nervous tic or something?"

"Of course not," he said, then screwed up his face in annoyance, because that's exactly what it was. Damn, for someone who supposedly didn't socialize much, the woman had picked up on one of his most obvious tells.

The involuntary gesture was the reason he'd had to grow his beard when he played baseball, making it appear as though he was simply smoothing down his facial hair rather than alerting the opposition to his discomfort. But he wasn't about to admit that to her. "Actually, ever since a woman tried to give me the Heimlich maneuver and then pointed out that I had spinach stuck in my teeth, I've been a little self-conscious about having something on my face."

Her face grew red. "I am so sorry about that. I really did think you were choking." There was a note of insecurity in her voice, and he cursed himself for being the cause of it. Especially since he'd made the joke to deflect from his habit of touching his former beard.

"Don't worry about it. Scooter and Jonesy thought it was hilarious. I don't suppose you have any plates packed away in one of those boxes?" he finally asked.

"Plates? Oh. Right." She tightened her already perfect ponytail. "I guess I'll need to get some of those, too. I've never had to furnish an entire house before, and I was so focused on getting the upstairs bedroom and bath livable, I didn't even think about how the rest would all come together."

Was she serious? She'd been studying for her med school entrance exams at the same age when he'd been studying for his driver's license test, yet she hadn't thought about the most basic necessities of a house. How could she be so naive?

"Most women I know wouldn't dream of moving into a house and roughing it without some long-term plan in place."

"Well, I'm not most women."

He forced himself not to look her up and down and confirm her obvious statement. Instead, he handed her a cold slice of pizza loaded with…what were those? Carrots? Who puts carrots on a pizza?

"Thank you," she said, looking anything but grateful to hold her food in her bare hands. Well, Just Julia should've thought that one out a bit more. Then he wanted to kick himself for being such an insensitive jerk. He took a bite of veggie-covered congealed cheese to keep himself from saying something he'd regret.

Big mistake, he realized when his throat refused to welcome a piece of broccoli. He coughed several times before getting the bite down. Then waved his hand at the concerned look on Julia's face. The last thing his extra tense, hyperaware muscles needed was for her to wrap her arms around his chest again.

"I'm okay. But would it have killed Freckles to order an extra pizza for your poor contractor? One with a little pepperoni and sausage?"

"Let me get you something to drink," Julia said, walking toward the grocery bag he'd dropped by the front door. She pulled out a yellow-green soda and twisted the top off for him.

He felt his eyebrows shoot up to his hairline. "You won't eat meat, but you'll drink that?"

"I know it's a contradiction, but growing up, I wasn't allowed to have any junk food. Yet I was able to convince my parents that it gave me an extra boost of energy so I could study longer."

Ma and Pa Fitzgerald sounded like a real barrel of fun, and again Kane found himself experiencing a sense of pity rather than inadequacy. As much as he hated the fact that his grades had prevented him from going to college, at least he'd had loving and supportive parents growing up.

He shook his head as Julia handed the drink to him.

The neon color was about the least healthy shade he'd ever seen, and he had to wonder if the genius gene had skipped a generation in her family. "No, thanks. If I drink that, I'll be up all night."

He picked off the more offending vegetables and threw them in the black trash bag he'd set up in the corner of the room. With nowhere to sit, they ate their cold meal standing up, Kane growing more and more restless by the second. By the time he'd gotten down to his third piece of crust, his legs were so fidgety, he'd begun pacing the room.

"It's getting pretty late," he finally said. "I'm going to run back upstairs and get my tools and stuff out of your room so you can get settled in."

"All right," she said, "I'm just going to wash my hands." He sure hoped she'd brought some soap with her.

Then the thought of soap made him think about bubbles, which made him think about her in the bath and...

Man, he needed to get out of here. He took the steps two at a time and grabbed his tool bag and portable speaker in record time. He was halfway out the front door when her voice stopped him.

"Do you think you could help me with a list?" she asked.

He froze. What list? The man list? Was she seriously asking for his help with something so personal? "Um. Depends."

His voice sounded like he still had broccoli stuck in his throat, and his once restless feet felt as though they were encased in concrete as he forced himself to turn and face her.

She bit her lower lip before explaining. "I'm only on call tomorrow, so I planned to go shopping as long as no emergencies come up. There are so many things I need for the house. I was hoping you could tell me what I should buy. I'd ask Freckles, but the café is usually packed on the weekends, and besides, she'd probably talk me into stocking up on a bunch of kitchen supplies I won't ever use."

Aw, hell. Kane knew his answer long before he said it. He'd been a protective older brother for too long, and he was instantly reminded of what her aunt had said about Julia being too trusting and needing someone more worldly to look out for her. Besides, he was going to be working here for a couple more months and could probably benefit from her having a better stocked kitchen.

"Sure, I'll make some notes and bring you a list tomorrow." Of course, that would mean a lot of writing and concentrating, and it would just be far easier if he went and picked up all the stuff at the store himself. He thought of something else Freckles had said about her niece's business sense. "You'll also need to get those appliances ordered."

"I know I've already asked so much of you, but do you think you could help me navigate that, too? After the whole furnace fiasco, I think I may need some refreshers on how to negotiate."

Kane clenched his jaw at the reminder. He'd wanted to kick that heating and air-conditioning salesman's ass for the price he'd quoted her last week. Instead, he'd called in one of his own subcontractors to do the installation. Sending Julia alone to one of those appliance warehouses would be like throwing her to the wolves.

"You know, my shoulder will probably still be a little sore tomorrow," he said, rotating it, this time not trying to hide his wince. "And I doubt I'll be able to get those cabinets in with just one good arm. Maybe I should go to that appliance place in Boise with you, and we can stop by one of those big department stores afterward and get you some of the basics you might need."

"Oh my gosh. I would appreciate that so much. Are you sure you won't mind?" He'd mind more if he had to watch her be taken advantage of by some salivating salesmen looking to pad their commissions. And it would keep him from having to write out a list of his own. Really, it was a win-win. As long as he managed not to touch her. Or smell her shampoo. Or look at her sexy lips.

Man, his senses were out of control. Especially his common sense.

"I'll pick you up at eight." His voice sounded a bit more gruff than he'd intended.

He saw her peek around him and look out the front door at his Bronco before saying, "Why don't I drive? After all, it's not fair for you to have to use up your gas money on an errand for me."

Gas money? Did she think he was some broke guy down on his luck?

"Besides," she continued before he could take too much offense at the assumption he was purposely hoping people would make about him. "You should give your shoulder some rest, and steering on those steep mountain curves will do more harm than good." She tossed the crust of her pizza into the trash, wiped her hands on a napkin and stood up. "All right, then. I'm going upstairs to soak in my new bathtub. See you tomorrow."

He blinked twice. Despite another awkward dismissal, he was touched that she was taking his well-being, and his gasoline budget, into account. He was also slightly annoyed by her presumption that he couldn't afford to take her somewhere and Kane didn't know how to reconcile his conflicting feelings.

He told himself that her concern was a refreshing

change from many of the women he'd dated in the past who seemed to be more interested in his celebrity status and seven-figure income than in him. Not that she was interested in dating him. But if Just Julia truly was clueless about who he was, then she was proving herself to be a thoughtful and kind person. Judging by her list and her determination to excel at everything, she'd make some guy damn lucky once she got herself settled.

Which was a good thing for him, as well. The sooner she got off the market, the sooner he'd be able to get her and her damn bathtub out of his mind.

Chapter Five

Kane was surprised that his six-foot-two body was able to scrunch into the passenger seat of Julia's MINI Cooper the following morning. He'd voiced his concern out loud when she'd walked out her front door carrying her key fob and another yellow-green soda for the road, yet she insisted that the inside of her car was deceptively roomy.

Kane had a thing about arguing with a determined woman so early in the day. He also had a thing about zippy little cars, especially the kind that didn't come with a six-figure price tag or a midlife crisis ego boost. His muscles were already clenching at the thought of being stuck in the passenger seat for the next hour or so. He didn't need the added stimulation of being this close to her out of her surgical uniform. Granted, she wasn't wearing the sexy workout gear, but her dark jeans encased her long, athletic legs and as she sat behind the wheel, her well-tailored blouse slightly gaped open where the top two buttons should've been fastened to prevent him from catching a glimpse of the curve of her left breast.

"How long have you had this?" he asked as he buckled his seat belt. He could still smell the faint traces of new car scent.

"I bought it about four months ago," Julia said, proudly smiling as if she'd just told him it was her first Nobel Prize. They had those things for doctors, didn't they? "I've never owned a car before. Or at least, a car that didn't come with a hired driver."

His brain picked up the clue to her implied wealthy background, and maybe he'd remember that tidbit of information later, but he could only focus on the more important admission that this was her very first car.

"What did you drive before this?" he asked.

"Oh, I didn't get my driver's license until I was stationed at Shadowview. I always lived in a city with a mass transit system or on a military base and never really had to drive anywhere before now."

She reached forward and tried to program something into the GPS system, but her thumb hit the speakerphone button. "Name, please," the electronic voice said.

"Directions to Boise," Julia called out, and Kane had to look out the passenger window so she couldn't see him trying not to laugh.

"Contact not recognized," the speakerphone replied.

Julia repeated the command again and got the same response. She shrugged and said, "I don't think the navigation system recognizes my voice."

"Let me try," Kane said, pushing the menu button before typing in the address.

"Calculating route," the electronic voice announced, and a map popped onto the screen.

"Thanks." Julia smiled, then snapped her seat belt

into place. "There's supposedly an instructional video to learn how to use that thing, but I haven't exactly had time to take a look at it. Yet."

Everything was *yet* with this woman. He studied her from behind the dark lenses of his Ray-Bans, while she fiddled with the radio dial, sending the volume skyrocketing and forcing Kane to cover his ears.

"Sorry," she said. "I'm still getting the hang of this stereo system, too."

"Is there an instructional video for that, as well?" he murmured, but because her finger had accidentally hit the mute button at that exact second, she ended up hearing him.

"Probably. But I might have to look online for it. With the house remodel and taking on some of Captain Karim's patients while he's on deployment, I just haven't had any extra time. But I'll figure it out eventually."

They set out down Pinecone Court. Julia was in fact a better driver than he'd expected, considering the way she handled her smartphone and the other devices in the small, well-equipped car. But by the time they were heading south on Snowflake Boulevard, Kane's left knee was doing its hummingbird imitation and he had to use his hand to hold it steady. He should've insisted on driving. Focusing on the road would've given him something to do. Being the driver gave him freedom to be in control of the car, of something bigger than him. He was a horrible passenger because he felt like a prisoner, trapped.

When she reached for the thermostat controls, he practically pushed her hand out of the way before she could accidentally set the seat warmer on high. "Let me help you with that so you can concentrate on driving."

"Thanks, but I've got it. I'm a surgeon, remember? My hands are used to multitasking."

He stared at her palms placed precisely at the ten and two positions. She might have phenomenal surgical skills, but her inability to master electronics was making his own fingers twitch with the need to commandeer something. Anything. Man, he hated just sitting here, being this far away from the steering wheel.

"So, why neurology?" he asked, his eyes squeezed tightly shut behind his sunglasses. Not that he was one for idle chitchat—or any kind of chitchat, really—but if they were going to be stuck in this car that he couldn't drive with a radio she couldn't operate, he might as well get the woman talking about herself before she decided to ask him any personal questions.

"Because it's the hardest," Julia said.

"You mean, it's hard working with patients who have so much to lose?"

"Well, that, too, I guess. But I meant it was one of the more intellectually challenging medical specialties. The central nervous system is the control pad that makes all the other body parts function."

He didn't want to point out that in the few times he'd been around her, she hadn't exactly been all that great with any other types of control pads. Instead he asked, "You chose your specialty because you wanted to be at the top of the field, not because you have a special affinity for the brain?"

"Well, of course I'm fascinated by the brain. And the cerebrovascular system. I mean, who wouldn't be?"

Kane wanted to raise his hand and claim, *Me! I wouldn't be fascinated by any of that.*

"Kind of sounds like you're a bit of an overachiever," Kane suggested and saw her fingers tense up on the wheel. Whoops. "Uh, did I say something wrong?"

"No," she answered. "I guess I'm just a little sensitive to that word."

"To what word? *Overachiever?*"

"Yes. I know that being a child genius may sound all unique and fun, but it also has its drawbacks."

Actually, it didn't sound fun at all. It sounded like a lot of weight to carry in the expectations department. "What kind of drawbacks?" Kane asked.

"Being teased by older kids who are embarrassed that you scored higher than them on the AP Calculus exam or that you got into a better college. I know it's just jealousy on their part, but it can wear on a person after a while."

A warm dart of sympathy shot through Kane's rib cage. "I wasn't making fun of you. I meant *overachiever* as a compliment. You're talking to someone who took typing as an elective, even though I can't spell worth a damn, because the wood shop teacher made students write essays on the different species of wood."

"But if you enjoy being a contractor, why wouldn't you want to excel at it? It would be such a waste not to try, at least."

Kane rolled his shoulder against the tight restraint of the seat belt and thought about his own waste of talent now that his athletic career was over. Her words were hitting home better than any coach's ever could. In baseball, he was notorious for going against the best and beating the odds. He used to revel in the challenge, in the competition. So why did he always take a backseat to real life when it became too difficult?

"Speaking of careers," he said, hoping she would be too polite to say anything about his cop out of a response. "Why did you join the Navy?" he asked.

"My parents were in a train crash when I was twenty-one. My mom died at the scene, but my father was in the

ICU for several days before he passed. I was sitting in the waiting room, and a documentary came on about the WAVES, the naval reserve for women during World War II. I was completely fascinated. Really, I was fascinated by all the shows I saw in there because I'd never been allowed to watch much television growing up, but the series on the WAVES really made me think that I could dedicate my brain and my knowledge to something besides science. Here were all these women who'd volunteered to go into the military for the good of the country rather than for personal gain, and I wanted to be like them. I wanted to help others."

She was not only a genius but also a damn do-gooder. How could he compete with someone like that? Not that they were in competition, but if they were, he wouldn't even be in the same league.

"I'm sorry about your parents," Kane offered, not knowing what else to say without pointing out more of his own inadequacies.

"Thank you." She'd reverted to that formal, stiff tone that made him want to tell her to stop being so damn proper. At least not for his benefit. "Aunt Freckles suggested I not make any big decisions while I was still grieving, but I was so used to the schedule my parents had set for me that I thought the order and discipline and routine of the Navy would actually be a comfort."

Hmm. Those were the same reasons Kane *hadn't* joined the military. He'd had a hard enough time following orders in high school. In fact, baseball was the only team sport he could manage because, as a pitcher, he was able to be somewhat on his own. Kane scratched at his chin, mentally calculating how much longer he would be stuck in this seat.

"Has anyone ever told you that you're very fidgety?" she asked when she finally hit the off-ramp.

"Only when I don't like sitting still."

"Hmm. Interesting," she said, reminding him of a therapist making notes in a patient's file. Kane should've known nothing good would come of them going into town together, but last night he'd let his mouth engage before his brain. He was still pretty sensitive about his childhood diagnosis and would've asked if she was trying to assess him. But he preferred that she focus all of her concentration on her third attempt to reenter their destination address after she'd accidentally switched off the navigation system when she'd picked up her bottle of soda.

He could offer to show her how to do it again, but he had the feeling Dr. Smarty-Pants wouldn't like the implication that she couldn't accomplish something herself after the first try. It was going to be a long day.

As the automatic glass doors swished open, Julia watched Kane pull his green ball cap lower until the brim nearly touched his sunglasses, which he didn't seem inclined to put away once they entered the store. She'd worked alongside plenty of men in the Navy, but that didn't mean she understood when one was being so frustratingly moody. Or secretive. What was up with his whole stealth disguise? He was one video camera still away from looking like a convenience store robber at large.

"Hello, and welcome to Land O'Appliances." A large voice boomed out from an even larger man dressed in a trendy pastel button-up shirt. The name tag pinned crookedly over the man's orange paisley tie read Paulie. Julia immediately took a step back, bumping into Kane's injured shoulder. The only things louder than Paulie's greeting and his taste in neckwear were the painful-looking injection sites from what her medical training told her was a recently botched Botox treatment.

"Is there anything in particular I can help you two find?" the salesman asked.

She looked at Kane, waiting for him to tell Paulie what they'd come to buy. But her quiet contractor said nothing, one hand gripping a half-used notepad and the other shoved deep inside the front pocket of his jeans. While Julia was accustomed to taking charge in classrooms or in surgery, she wasn't as experienced as she would have liked when it came to negotiating.

"I need a new refrigerator," Julia finally said to the eager salesman with his bleached white smile, before shooting Kane an imploring look to chime in. She couldn't very well be rude and just stand there saying nothing.

"Well, you've come to the right place," Paulie said. She tried not to flinch at his volume, which hadn't lowered when he came closer. "All our fridges are back against this wall. Do you have a price in mind?"

"Oh, I suppose we're more concerned with the style than the pri—"

"We want inexpensive," Kane interrupted. So *now* he decided to grace them with his input. Then he raised his rudeness another level when he told Paulie, "We'll take a look around and let you know if we have any questions."

Kane lightly gripped her elbow and steered her toward the refrigerator department. She caught the scent of spicy shower gel and coffee when he leaned in close to her and whispered, "When you're negotiating, never tell the opposing side that you're not concerned with the price."

Manners had been instilled in Julia since before she

could speak, which was why she cast a nervous look over her shoulder to the abandoned salesman before directing her quiet reply toward the plaid-patterned flannel covering Kane's shoulder. "But we weren't at the negotiating part yet."

"We were at the negotiating part the second we walked in the door and Paulie Loudmouth over there was calculating how many extra tanning bed sessions he could buy with our commission."

"I didn't realize you knew the employees here already."

"I don't," Kane said. "But all these salespeople are the same."

"Then why didn't you take the lead when he approached us?"

"I did."

"How? By being rude and not saying a word?"

"I wasn't being rude. I was being hard to read. If I came in looking like an eager beaver, Paulie would've had us right where he wanted us."

"I see," she said, not seeing at all but willing to go along with his reverse psychology strategy. For now.

He didn't release her arm as he successfully maneuvered her in front of a nondescript white unit that didn't even have an ice maker. While she wasn't used to being touched—or, some might argue, manhandled—so intimately, she didn't attempt to pull away. But only because she didn't want to thwart what might be part of his negotiation tactic. It certainly wasn't because she liked the feel of his strong fingers through the thin cotton of her white blouse.

"But Kane, I don't want to look at these plain refrigerators. I thought we agreed that the stainless steel ones over there would look better with the granite countertops."

"Don't point," he said as he dropped her elbow, causing her tummy to sink in disappointment. He reached across to pull her pointing hand back, and his bare forearm brushed across her chest. Julia's cheeks flooded with heat as her nipples tightened in response. Logically, she knew the movement was inadvertent on his part, but that didn't stop her from feeling as though an electric current had been shot through her body.

Thankfully, Kane must not have noticed her reaction to his touch because Mr. Controlling Contractor leaned in and gave her another order under his breath. "Make them think we're interested only in the cheaper models. He'll still try to upsell us, but his expectations won't be as high."

Oh, for the love of all things good. She'd asked for Kane's support and experience. Not for his high-handedness or a lesson in power-play maneuvers. And she especially hadn't asked for his full lips to practically caress her temple as he whispered in her ear.

She'd never been so aware of a man's nearness and tried to chalk this overpowering sensation up to her inexperience in being in this type of situation.

But just because she'd never been shopping for appliances before didn't mean she couldn't figure out how it was done.

"Kane, this is a store. Not a fine art auction house. There are huge price tags on everything. Clearly there's a set price. So let's just pick the one we want and pay for it."

"Come on, Dr. Smarty-Pants. This isn't how businesses like these operate."

"What did you just call me?" She turned toward him and crossed her arms, not sure if she was more offended by the nickname or by the implication that she wasn't capable of doing something so simple as buying a refrigerator.

"Sorry. I meant it as a compliment." He did that little smirk thing again, not even having the decency to look sheepish or remorseful.

"Smarty-pants? Overachiever?" She put her hands on her hips, trying to figure out if he was patronizing her or if this was how friends teased each other. "You sure have a funny way of delivering a compliment."

"Can we shelve the arguments right now? Paulie is walking this way to check on us, and we need to appear to be on the same team."

Julia thought they *were* on the same team. Until he'd started "complimenting" her. Something about his teasing tone triggered that underlying desire in her to prove that she wasn't completely in the dark. Perhaps it might benefit him to realize a little something about his so-called teammate. "I'll have you know that I took a global business concepts course my sophomore year in college."

One side of his mouth quirked up, making her brain go all fuzzy and forget why she'd been so annoyed with him a second ago. "I'm guessing that, based on your recent history with the furnace, you aced that class."

Oh yeah. His sarcasm was why.

"It was more theory than practical approach, but I still passed," she whispered out the side of her mouth right as the salesman arrived, glad she didn't have to admit that her passing score was the lowest one on her undergrad transcripts.

"I saw the missus pointing to one of our most popular models," Paulie said as he walked up. He attempted a wink, but the Botox in his forehead made the gesture seem more like a mild focal seizure. "Everyone is buying stainless steel these days."

"Oh no, I'm not the… I mean not *his*…" Julia broke off when she saw Kane pull his sunglasses off—finally— and pinch the bridge of his nose. Maybe she should've stuck with being on Kane's team, but she didn't want to give anyone the impression that they were a couple. Or together…in *that* way. It would've been misleading. Mostly to her. And she'd learned long ago not to be misled by a man who wasn't actually interested in a serious relationship.

"Here's the thing, Paulie." Kane shoved the sunglasses in his shirt pocket, and Julia tried not to stare at the slight rise of his pectoral muscle underneath. Was it getting warmer in here? "We're remodeling a house and are actually in the market for several kitchen appliances, as well as a washer and dryer. Now, I have a pretty good idea of what models and styles are going to work best, so we don't really need your assistance in that regard. However, my *missus* and I will require your help in making sure we get the best deal. Think you can do anything to help us out?"

Julia would've pointed out how ridiculous Kane's lie was if his words hadn't made Paulie's collagen-plumped lips smile in anticipation.

Or if his reference to her being his "missus" hadn't made her legs buckle and her heart beat so hard, she could feel it pulsing behind her unblinking eyes.

Chapter Six

Julia walked out of Land O'Appliances with the promise of a Monday delivery and the loss of her car keys. She wasn't quite sure how her moody contractor had been smooth or charming enough to manage either. She blamed her easy acquiescence and light-headedness on the fact that she'd skipped breakfast.

"Are you hungry?" she asked Kane as they walked toward her car.

"I'm always hungry." He pulled that gold watch out his pocket and flipped it open. His use of the antique timepiece struck her as such a stunning contrast to his rugged construction worker look. "Besides, it's almost eleven, so we have time to grab something before we hit Bed Bath & Beyond."

"Great. You brought the shopping list, I hope? We can go over it while we eat."

"Don't need a list," he said, pointing to the side of his head. "I've got it all up here."

Julia would have rolled her eyes at his confident bragging, but she was too busy trying to pull up the restaurant locator app Chief Wilcox had downloaded to her phone last week.

"What are you doing?"

"Trying to find a place to eat." She showed him the screen. "See, it recommends the Aztec Taqueria, which is only a few hundred yards from here on Callejon Road."

"Julia, I'm pretty sure there isn't a Callejon Road around this part of Boise."

"Yes, there is." She pointed to the small map. "We're the blue dot right here next to it."

The sound of Kane's deep, rumbling laughter shocked her, then sent an unexpected vibration through her bloodstream. "What's so funny?"

"You have the current location set for Taos, New Mexico."

She was relieved that the man actually had a sense of humor buried somewhere deep inside his aloof shell, but that didn't stop the back of her neck from bristling with embarrassment that he was actually laughing *at* her. Or was it tingling at the sight of his straight, white teeth flashing with actual mirth?

"Whatever," she said, slipping the dumb phone back into her purse. "That restaurant across the parking lot looks like a good place to eat. And it's close enough to walk."

"The Bacon Palace?" He raised one of his auburn eyebrows at her, and Julia decided she liked quiet, brooding Kane much better than smug, teasing Kane. "I thought you were a vegetarian."

Gulp. "Oh, I'm sure they'll have something there that will suit me just fine."

Of course, judging by the sizzling aroma wafting across the asphalt as Julia walked beside him, she had a feeling the words *hold the bacon* would be an addendum to her order.

Kane held open the pink door painted to look like a pig's snout and Julia kept her opinions about the swine-themed decor and the misleading signage to herself. The proprietors got half of the restaurant's name correct, but this place was definitely no palace.

After making a pretense of intently studying the trough-shaped wooden menu above the cash register—she'd had no idea that a breakfast meat could flavor everything from pasta sauces to milkshakes—Julia ordered a basket of plain french fries and a garden salad, minus the bacon ranch dressing. She pulled out her wallet before Kane finished ordering his triple-stacked BLT and handed her American Express card to the cashier.

"No," Kane said. "You're not paying for my lunch."

"Well, you're certainly not paying for *my* lunch. It's not like this is a date."

His eyelids lowered as though he was trying understand a foreign language. "I'm not poor, you know."

"I never said you were," she replied, then walked over to the soda machine so he couldn't see that her cheeks were the same shade as the pink plastic drink cup she'd just grabbed. Had she messed up? Had she offended his pride? Ugh. It was times like this when she hated her social awkwardness.

This was why she was single. She couldn't even carry on a normal conversation with a man she wasn't dating. A man she wasn't the slightest bit interested in. Attracted to, maybe, but that wasn't the same thing. Which was why Julia had made that comment about this not being a date. More to remind herself of the fact since, judging by his annoyed expression, Kane Chatterson certainly didn't need reminding.

In fact, he didn't say another word as they sat down across from each other at a small booth in the crowded restaurant. She'd heard his laughter outside only briefly, and though it had been at her expense, she regretted that it had been short-lived. Julia was accustomed to being on her own, and silence was pretty much standard in her house growing up. So she didn't mind him not speaking. But she hated the fact that she might've offended Kane or done something to ruin the good mood he'd been in a few minutes ago.

"Are you okay?" she finally asked when he didn't say more than two words to the friendly server who'd brought them their food.

"I don't like big crowds," he said before hunkering down over his plate and taking a large bite of his sandwich.

Then it *wasn't* her or something she'd said. She was no expert on cognitive behavior therapy, but perhaps if she got his mind on something else, he would be able to relax and enjoy the meal, at least.

"So, you were in the military," she started, thinking they could discuss something they had in common.

His brows shot up. "No. Why would you think that?"

"Because I saw you at Shadowview. Why would you be a patient there if you weren't a veteran or on active duty?"

"What makes you think I'm a patient?"

Julia couldn't very well ask him why he was in the psych department the other day. Perhaps he'd been there visiting someone, but she could have sworn that the room he'd gone to was where the PTSD group held their sessions. She squirmed slightly in her seat. "No reason."

Sharing a meal with such an attractive man—even in a location such as the Bacon Palace, of all places—wasn't something that happened to her all that often, and this was why. She didn't have anything to talk to a good-looking man about. Julia picked up a french fry, racking her brain for another conversation starter. But before she was forced to ask him about the wainscoting in her downstairs bathroom, she recognized another doctor from the base hospital coming toward their table.

"Kane, it's good to see you out and about," Dr. Drew Gregson said as he reached out to shake Kane's hand.

"Shh, Drew." Kane pulled his hat lower and sank deeper into the vinyl booth seat. "Do you have to be so loud?"

She had met the Navy psychologist at the hospital during one of the bigger admin meetings and seemed to recall that he also lived near Sugar Falls. But that didn't explain why Julia's surly contractor was on such familiar terms with him. Unless they were encouraged to use first names in those PTSD sessions.

"Sorry. I guess I was just surprised to see you making a rare public appearance." The psychologist, who'd inadvertently just given Julia some insight into the man spending every day working on her home, turned to her. "Hi. I'm Drew Gregson."

"I know," Julia said, returning his handshake. "We both work at Shadowview."

The man took off his wire-framed glasses, probably fogged up by the bacon-tinged air around them, and wiped them off. She didn't blame him for not recognizing her out of uniform and without her standard surgical scrubs.

"Julia Fitzgerald. I'm in Neurology."

"Of course. That's right. Kane's remodeling that old Victorian on Pinecone Court for you, right?"

Apparently Kane told his therapist all kinds of information about himself. Maybe she should ask Dr. Gregson for some tips on how to get the man to open up more when he was with her.

Wait. Where did that thought come from? She didn't want Kane Chatterson opening up to her about anything but carpet samples and light fixtures. It was already bad enough that her heart rate accelerated every time his lips gave off the slightest grin. She'd probably suffer from a full blown case of tachycardia if he actually engaged in a friendly conversation.

Julia gave him an exaggerated nod, trying to shake loose the unwarranted analysis of her contractor's personality. "That's right. We came into Boise to pick out some appliances, and Kane was kind enough to offer me his expertise at Bed Bath & Beyond next."

Julia wanted to make their relationship sound as businesslike and professional as possible. But something about the other doctor's quirked smile made her think she'd done just the opposite.

"Is that so?" Gregson asked. "My twin brother and his fiancée, Carmen, just registered at Bed Bath & Beyond for their wedding gifts. I'm sure Luke would've loved your *expertise* with that, Kane."

Julia wasn't positive, but she could've sworn Kane's shoulders visibly shuddered at the word *wedding*. She wiped her mouth on the pink paper napkin—seriously, pink?—and pushed her salad plate away. If there was any other way to signal it was time to exit this odd conversation, she didn't know how to go about it.

"You know what else I'm an expert at?" Kane spoke

so low, Julia didn't know if it was annoyance in his tone or something more sinister. "Taking all your winnings at poker. Get ready to pay up next Thursday, doc."

When Dr. Gregson let out a loud burst of laughter, Julia finally released the breath she'd been holding, feeling more out of place than she had back in the appliance store.

Today was a perfect example of the reason Kane avoided cities, shaved his beard and kept his hat firmly in place—even when he was indoors. He didn't want to be recognized. Of all the people they had to run into at a crowded restaurant, why did it have to be his know-it-all brother-in-law? And what was up with Just Julia's insistence on paying for lunch for him?

Was she under some impression that Kane was poor? First she'd paid for his breakfast at the Cowgirl Up when she thought he'd been choking. Then she'd made that comment about not wanting him to use his own gas money to drive into the city. And just a few minutes ago, she'd swiped her credit card before he even had a chance to do the gentlemanly thing and offer to pay. He hadn't had a woman pay for one of his meals since…well, since ever. Not that he and Julia were on a date or anything, which she'd made more than clear. But still.

It had felt cheap. As though he was simply the hired help—which he was currently acting like as he pushed the nearly full shopping cart behind her down the kitchen gadget aisle of the big home goods store.

Worker, employee, someone to pay. That's what he was to her, after all. What he *should* be. Hell, they weren't even friends, which was too bad, because the woman's rear end looked more than friendly in those expensive, curve-hugging dark jeans. His chest tightened and for the hundredth time that day, he asked himself why couldn't she have worn her boxy hospital scrubs. Kane was no expert on women's fashion, but today, Julia's outfit was serving up one contradiction after another. Her clothes were simple, but obviously high quality. Preppy, but sexy at the same time. Like she wasn't trying to flaunt her good looks, but they were still so obviously there. It was distracting, and he'd been having a difficult time keeping his eyes off her. Worse, it drew too much attention to her from other people.

Not that he cared if slick salesmen or overeager waiters were checking her out. The problem was that it also drew attention to *him*. Kane ran his fingers under his bottom lip. Erica used to love it when they'd get all dressed up for a dinner event or a fancy cocktail party with the team owners. Once Kane had been horrified to overhear her telling the cameraman to make sure to capture everyone's reactions when the hottest couple in the sports celebrity world walked into the room. Once upon a time, he hadn't minded the attention to his skills on the mound, but he'd never been comfortable with being recognized in public. Now, he simply avoided it at all costs.

"Do you think seven hundred dollars is too much to pay for a set of knives?" Julia had her back toward him, her cute blond ponytail bouncing as she took in the variety of displays. "Maybe they'd be willing to give us some sort of discount, like Paulie did over at Land O'Appliances."

"Jules, this isn't the kind of place where you can negotiate prices." *Jules?* He squeezed his eyes shut in an effort to clear his mind. Where had that name come from? Like most of the stupid things he'd said in his life, it'd impulsively popped out before he could think about the inappropriateness of giving his client a nickname.

"Of course it's not," she said, not noticing his slip, he hoped. "Even I know that. What I meant was that maybe they offer some sort of coupon or sale on certain items. Anyway, Aunt Freckles says to never scrimp on kitchen equipment, but I have no idea if this is a fair price. What do you think? Would you pay seven hundred dollars for 'VG-10 supersteel blades with durable pakkawood handles'? It says they were handcrafted in Japan."

"I wouldn't pay that much if they came with four wheels and their own engine."

"No, I don't suppose you would." She picked up the midprice brand instead and put it into the shopping cart on top of the sixteen-piece glassware set she'd selected twenty minutes ago.

There she went again, thinking he couldn't afford something, and a knot of shame wedged itself in his throat. What with his poor grades, his career-ending injury and being cheated on by his ex-girlfriend, Kane had experienced plenty of embarrassing moments in his life. But having a lack of money had never been the subject of any of his pity parties. In fact, he had almost as much money as he did pride, which was why he didn't want her thinking he was just some busted, broke-down contractor who couldn't pay for his own meals or buy his own set of fancy Shun double-bevel blades.

"Actually, I think you should get the nicer ones. Your Aunt Freckles would have a fit if she thought I was letting you purchase substandard tools." When he saw the doubt fill her green eyes, he said, "In fact, consider it a housewarming gift from me."

"Oh no. I couldn't accept such a generous gift from you."

He thought about the limited-edition Bentley he'd bought for Erica—before he found out she'd been sleeping with his nemesis while Kane was undergoing shoulder surgery. "Trust me. It's not that generous a gift."

"No, you don't understand. It would be wasted on me. I spend hardly any time in the kitchen. My aunt inherited all the culinary skills in the family. She wouldn't even let me help her slice peaches in the café last August when she was perfecting her recipe for the Cobbler Festival or one of those dessert themed events Sugar Falls always seems to be putting on."

"Maybe she thinks you need more practice with sharp instruments?"

"Are you kidding? I use scalpels and bone-cutting saws with as much precision as a laser. In fact, I use lasers, too. Steady hands, remember?" She placed her palms up, and he tightened his gut to keep from laughing at how unsteady those fingers had been at programming touch screens. Who in the world would've let this woman anywhere near a laser?

"All the more reason you should own a good set of knives," he said, sincerely hoping she wielded the sharp tools better than she operated a cell phone. "Speaking of Freckles, when I went in for breakfast this morning, Monica, that new waitress she hired, told me she was gone for the day. That's three Saturdays in a row that I haven't had my chicken-fried steak made the way I like."

"I think she might have a boyfriend," Julia whispered as though the thought of Freckles dating was some big secret. It wasn't.

"Is that a bad thing?"

"Not for her, no. But she thinks everyone should be paired off. In fact, she told me I needed to bring a date to the Sugar and Shadow Shindig next month."

"What in the hell is that?"

"Apparently, it's some annual fund-raiser dinner and

dance that the town puts on to benefit the hospital. Get it? Sugar Falls and Shadowview? I think it's supposed to be a play on words."

"Oh, I get it all right. I just hadn't heard that was the theme the committee had come up with for it this year."

"So you're familiar with it." Julia's eyes lit up, reflecting a hundred questions that Kane did *not* want to answer. "Are you going?"

"No way," he shook his head. "I stay far, far away from those kinds of dog and pony shows."

"Normally, I do, too." Julia leaned forward as though she were confiding in him. "But my commanding officer said that most of the doctors are expected to attend. Even if it wasn't a work-related function, Aunt Freckles would want me there so she could introduce me to most of the town all at once. I don't know if you've noticed, but my great-aunt can be a bit of a show-off."

"Yeah, it's hard not to notice. So…uh…have you found a date yet?" There he went, engaging his mouth before his brain again. He had no business asking her such a personal question, especially when his lungs froze as he waited for her answer.

"Pshh." She swatted her hand in the air. "Are you kidding? I barely have enough free time to go to a Laundromat, let alone go out looking for man. But I'll get to it."

"Huh." Kane leaned on the handle of the cart, struggling not to show his relief. "I'm surprised Aunt Freckles isn't doing your laundry for you."

Julia sighed. "She offered to. Unfortunately, she'd also spearhead the Find Julia a Man Committee if I'd let her."

Kane started to rub his chin, then thought better of it and pinched the bridge of his nose instead. "You're not going to let her, are you?"

"Do my laundry or set me up with a date for the hospital gala?"

"Either."

"Listen, if it were up to me, I'd be happy living alone and doing everything on my own. However, I promised my aunt I'd try to become a little more social, which isn't exactly one of my strengths. Yet."

With that, Julia moved toward the bedding section, and Kane walked beside her with enough questions to fill the shopping cart he was pushing. Personally, he didn't blame her one bit for not wanting to get dressed up and schmooze with all the bigwigs from the hospital. But he also understood about high-handed family members who thought they had your best interests at heart. While Kane could hold his own with the rest of the Chattersons, he doubted Julia would be tough enough to oppose her aunt. Hell, Kane himself had a hard time standing up to a determined Freckles. But there must be something he could do to help the underdog. He might not be great at studying, but he'd always been good at coming up with ways to fix things.

"Do you have a plan in mind?" he asked.

She stared at a shelving display and tapped her bow-shaped upper lip, making his mouth go dry. "I think the plan is to hold off on the new sheets until I order a real bed. But I might need a down comforter for my air mattress in the meantime."

"No, I meant do you have an idea of how you're going to get out of the Sugar and Shadow Shenanigans?"

"You mean the dance?" she corrected him, but a smile twitched at the corners of her lips. "Of course I'm not. Why would I try to get out of it?"

"Because you supposedly have a high IQ?"

Julia crossed those arms primly across her fitted white

blouse, making Kane's veins pulse at the sight of her breasts pushing up against the fabric.

"I'm assuming that you don't plan on attending," she said as though he was beneath fund-raising galas. Or maybe he was just being extra sensitive since his energy level was at an all-time high. His teeth ached from clenching together so tightly. "Don't get me wrong, I wish I could be like you and write the whole thing off. But the way I see it is that it's something I have to do. I might as well give it my best shot to find a date and try to make the evening a success."

Kane forced his jaw muscles to loosen. "It must be so easy to decide to master something and then snap your fingers and, boom, it happens."

She tilted her head and squinted. "I didn't say it was easy. In fact, I know I've got my work cut out for me. I just haven't found the time to put the effort into it. But I've set a goal for myself, and I've even made a list."

"A list? Of what?"

"Of…" She hesitated. "Of what I'd want in a date."

Oh no. Kane tugged his ball cap lower on his head. He really didn't want to think about what was on that stupid piece of paper again. Or the fact that he didn't meet any of those qualifications. But the impulsive demon inside him was overriding his common sense. Besides, it didn't help that they were standing in the middle of an aisle full of plush bedding and all he could think about was her bedroom. "What's on the list?"

Julia blushed, a deep scarlet to match the rose-printed decorative shams on display. "Just a little of this and that."

She was normally so confident, he felt his lips quirk at seeing her a bit flustered. But he also didn't want her thinking he was applying to be her date. At least not the kind her aunt would approve of. His eyes lowered to her soft pink lips and he briefly toyed with the idea of putting on a tux and taking her to the gala himself if it meant he'd get a good-night kiss.

Her head was tilted up and it would be so easy to slide his hand around her neck and pull her toward him…

He took a step back, bumping into a stack of fleece blankets. He needed to lighten this discussion up, fast, before he did something stupid. "Forget the details. So you make the ideal-man list. And then what? You go out shopping for a guy like you would a refrigerator?"

Julia inhaled deeply, then tested the satiny softness of a down-filled pillow above her head. The motion caused her shirt to pull against her chest again, and he saw the faint outline of her lace bra underneath. Maybe they should make their way to the bath department to look at something less inviting. Like toilet plungers.

"Wouldn't that be nice and simple?" she said, a dreamy look on her face. "I could just bring in my notepad and show it to Paulie, the salesman, and poof!" She snapped her fingers. "He could fix everything for me. No more being the wallflower and not fitting in at parties."

Kane would've been saddened by her words if his blood wasn't pumping in disgust over the thought of someone fake and phony like Paulie Loudmouth seeing to her needs. Which led to him thinking about the slimy salesman or some another jerk sharing that pillow with her. Taking advantage of her natural innocence. Her naïveté with people could really get her into trouble in a dating situation…

The runaway train of thought made his chest constrict with concern—and his lungs fill with jealousy. And before he could consider what he was saying, Kane heard himself suggest, "You know, I could help you find a guy."

Chapter Seven

Thankfully, Julia's cell phone rang and she'd been called in to assist with a complicated emergency surgery seconds after he'd made the impulsive offer. Well, not thankfully for Corporal Rosenthal, who had been touch and go for a while after the removal of the blood clot in his brain. But at least she'd been saved the embarrassment of taking Kane up on his offer to find her a plus-one for the hospital gala.

Especially after she'd caught him staring at her lips in the bedding aisle and had held her breath, hoping he would volunteer to go as her date. Oh, who was she kidding? Standing so close to him, she'd been hoping he'd offer a lot more than that.

But he hadn't even touched her, let alone kissed her, and the hollowness of disappointment was just as fresh several hours later.

Julia stood in the middle of the officers' locker room,

stretching out the muscles in her lower back. When she got the call earlier today...wait. She looked at the clock on the wall. It was after oh four hundred. Make that yesterday. When she'd gotten the emergency call *yesterday*, Kane had abandoned the loaded shopping cart in an empty aisle and had driven her straight to the hospital. He didn't say a word—not that he could've spoken much since she'd been on the phone getting briefed by the head ER doctor—and she hadn't allowed herself to think about anything beyond what awaited her in the operating room.

In fact, Julia wasn't even sure what had happened to her car until she'd gotten out of surgery and saw his text message, before she'd accidentally deleted it. Apparently he'd parked it in long-term parking and called for a ride home. The fact that he'd volunteered to help her "find a guy" made it pretty clear that he was of the same mindset she was when it came to dating. Or at least, when it came to dating her. Still, after with the deal he'd gotten on her appliances yesterday, as well as the extra time he'd had to put in, she found herself in Kane's debt once again.

Julia wondered who he possibly could've called to pick him up at the base hospital. Sure, he probably had a family or maybe even friends nearby. But he seemed like even more of a loner than she was. Which made it all the more odd that he thought he could help her find a suitable date. Actually, he'd never said suitable. Her mind flashed back to the angry old cowboy he'd been arguing with in the Cowgirl Up Café that morning he'd acted like he was being poisoned by vegetables. She could only imagine what kind of guy Kane would come up with on his own.

And that brought her back to her original thought. Her emergency call had saved her from having to decline his offer. Although she would decline it, eventually. If she could figure out a way to do it without making her sink

into a hole with shame. She was already having difficulty explaining to her Aunt Freckles about boundaries
and registering an online dating profile in Julia's name.
Misreading Kane's intentions and crossing the line of
professionalism was too big of a risk for her to take.

She took a quick shower before heading out to the
parking lot, where she'd found the key fob under the
front passenger-side tire, right where Kane's text said
it would be.

The leather interior smelled of his spicy, masculine
scent, and when she started the engine, the satellite radio
shot to life, the volume at a much higher decibel level than
any audiologist would recommend. The display screen
told her that Louis Jordan was playing on the jazz station.
Not that Julia was one to categorize people or rely on ste-
reotypes, but this was the second time she'd found herself surprised at the musical choice of a simple contractor
from a simple town. But she tapped her fingers against
the gearshift and let the piano and trombone melodies
carry her up the mountain toward Sugar Falls.

Kane was proving to be quite a contradiction of what
she'd first expected and she made a mental note to find
out more about him. After all, the last time she'd allowed
herself to be so naive about a man she'd been dating, Julia
had been devastated by the truth.

Wait. She and Kane weren't dating. They weren't even
friends. She forced her fingers to relax on the steering wheel
as she chastised herself for comparing her contractor—
who didn't owe her any explanations because she was not
in a relationship with him—to Stewart Morsely, who'd
purposely kept her in the dark about his real life.

Ella Fitzgerald was fittingly crooning when Julia was
at last turning off Snowflake Boulevard. The sun had
barely crested the twin pine trees behind her house, and

though she was relieved finally to be home, Julia sighed at the realization that she still needed to go back to the store and finish shopping today.

When she pulled into her driveway, she saw several cardboard boxes broken down and stacked next to her recycling bin. Upon closer inspection, she recognized the box from the knife set she'd wanted yesterday, as well as several others that had once contained measuring cups, dishes and even a KitchenAid stand mixer in pale blue.

Her cell phone rang, and she headed toward the front door, answering her aunt's call as she fumbled with her house keys. "Morning, Aunt Freckles."

"Morning, Sug. Did you get the introductory email from the An Apple a Day website?"

"Actually, I got it but I barely had time to glance at it."

"The ad said it's the premier dating service for singles in the medical profession. They even have a little apple-shaped app icon. We can download the app to your phone, and you can get suggested matches no matter where you are."

Julia didn't have the heart to point out her concerns with the marketing strategy behind naming a company after an old adage that promised to keep the doctor *away*. "I'll try to check it out when I get a moment."

"You don't *have* a lot of free moments, Sug. The gala is only a few weeks away. That's why I'm taking the liberty of speeding up this date-finding business for you." Oh great. It was a business now? "Anyway, I got your text yesterday about getting called into surgery and not being able to finish your shopping trip. You want me to come by this afternoon after the breakfast rush and we can have a second go-round?"

"Uh…hold that thought." Julia walked into her kitchen, the temporary sawhorse table cleaned off and the overhead cabinets snugly installed. She opened a cupboard door to find it filled with glasses. If Freckles hadn't gone back to the store to buy the stuff Julia had picked out, then who had?

She made her way into the butler's pantry and saw the top-of-the-line knife set sitting on a shelf, along with several other small appliances. There was a note next to the expensive-looking toaster that said "Put stuff in here till I get countertops installed. Maybe Monday." It wasn't signed, but she recognized Kane's scratchy handwriting.

"Sug? You still there?"

"Oh, yes. Sorry, Freckles. No, I don't need to go shopping today. It looks like Kane took care of it."

"You're kidding," her aunt said, and hearing the cackling laughter, Julia could almost picture the woman slapping her jeans-clad thigh. "I guess there's a lot more to that boy than a good throwing arm. No, Monica, those are the bowls for the fruit cups, not the oatmeal."

"Listen," Julia said, before her aunt became too engrossed in training the new waitress while she waited on the other end of the line. "I'm going to catch a little bit of sleep. Maybe you can tell me what you mean by 'good throwing arm' when we get together for dinner tonight?"

"Uh, tonight won't work for me," Freckles said, her voice pitched lower than normal. "I have, uh, plans."

Julia would've pressed her aunt for more details on what those plans might be—and whom they might involve—but she was still trying to figure out when Kane had time to play the home-goods fairy *and* install half of her kitchen cupboards.

So instead, she said goodbye, then fired off a quick text to the mysterious man. Did you buy all this?

She didn't get a response. It was then that she noticed someone had also made a run to Duncan's Market—the only grocery store in town—because one of the pantry shelves was stocked with cereal, crackers, granola bars, pasta and jars of gourmet vegetarian sauces.

Julia's sigh was almost as loud as the rumbling coming from her stomach. She would have to pay him back, of course, or maybe he'd bill her in a future invoice. Either way, she hadn't eaten since that meal at the Bacon Palace. She was excited just to have a bowl to pour some cereal into. Until she realized she still wouldn't have her refrigerator until it was delivered tomorrow. Which meant no milk.

Just then, she spied the cooler at the opposite end of the kitchen. Unless…nah…he wouldn't have taken the time to—yep. There was a quart of milk nestled on some fresh ice, along with a six-pack of her favorite soda.

Bless Kane Chatterson. Julia found a spoon in a silverware tray near the sink in the mudroom, which was the only functioning source of water downstairs. The man had even washed everything before putting it away. She was going to have to pay him a bonus.

She carried the bowl of raisin bran upstairs, trying not to wonder how he knew her preference for raisins, but stopped in her tracks when she saw a new down comforter spread out over her air mattress in the center of the bedroom. She knew she hadn't even made her bed before leaving the house yesterday. Mostly because it had been the first morning she'd woken up without a maid to do it for her or without a higher-ranking naval official directing her to do it.

But also because she was positive that she hadn't actually selected a comforter yesterday at the store. In fact, if she remembered correctly, she was still looking at sheets, thinking about kissing him, when Kane had made his impractical offer—which, suddenly, after Freckles's An Apple a Day suggestion, didn't seem so silly.

She looked at the crisp Egyptian cotton pillowcases covering what she suspected were brand-new fluffy pillows. Yet before she could think of the intimate implications of Kane Chatterson selecting her bedding, her cell phone rang again. She sat down at the edge of the air mattress as she spoke with the on-call neurologist who was following up on Corporal Rosenthal's care. After being reassured of her patient's condition, she didn't give her pillows or her inappropriate attraction to her handsome contractor another thought as she sank onto her freshly made bed and promptly fell asleep.

Kane saw Julia's text message when he woke up late Sunday morning. But he had a feeling she'd stayed up much later than he had, and he didn't want to disturb her with what was an obvious answer. Who else would have gone back to buy the stuff in her Bed Bath & Beyond cart and then spend all evening installing her overhead cupboards?

Not that he had anything better to do on a Saturday night. Two years ago around this time of day, he would've just been rolling in from a night of drinking and celebrating, catching a couple of hours of sleep before being expected to pitch the opening of a Sunday afternoon game. Once he committed to something, Kane didn't believe in doing anything half-assed. And partying had been no exception.

Not that he missed that particular aspect of his former life. In fact, toward the end of his career, he'd been spiraling more and more out of control. Like a foul ball spinning its way into the cheap seats. And he'd always known baseball wouldn't be forever. His body currently appreciated the slower pace of small-town life, but his restless mind sometimes needed more stimulation than what Sugar Falls had to offer.

He was itching to finish the lower kitchen cabinets at the Pinecone Court house, but he didn't want to disturb Julia if she was sleeping in. Plus, after that near kiss and his unexpected reaction to the thought of her dating, he didn't think it was a good idea to be too close to her right now. Knowing in his head that there was no way he'd actually act on his attraction was one thing. Communicating that rational thought to his nerve endings was another matter.

Just thinking about the way her lace bra had cupped the perfect shape of her breasts had Kane's palms sweating. Today it'd be much safer for him to get out of his house and do something that would get him refocused.

Maybe he'd go over to his sister's house, and offer to babysit his twin nieces. Or maybe he'd stop in at Russell's Sports and he and his buddy Alex could take a couple of the guys from the support group and a raft down the Sugar River rapids. Hell, if he really wanted to live dangerously, he could call up the nine-year-old Gregson twins—who technically were Drew's nephews, not his, but still called him Uncle Kane—and offer to take them on a mountain bike ride.

Deciding he needed a healthy dose of adrenaline and fear, he called Drew and made arrangements to do all three.

When Kane showed up at Julia's house on Monday morning, his injured shoulder should have been in a sling. But he'd swallowed down a few ibuprofens with his morning decaf and hauled his tool bag out of his backseat. Today, the kitchen would get done even if it killed him.

He needed to finish working on Dr. Smarty-Pants's house and move on to the next job. That way, he wouldn't be distracted by thoughts of her waking up wrapped up in that stupid down comforter he shouldn't have bought.

The basset hound he'd noticed the day she moved in was sitting on her front porch, and he moved toward the dog slowly, not knowing how friendly Julia's pet might be with strangers. He hadn't seen it that night he'd installed the overhead cupboards, but he wasn't paying attention to a lot of things lately. Or maybe Freckles took care of the animal when she was gone.

It let out a low growl. Kane, knowing he needed an ally if he was expected to work alongside the animal, reached into the white bag he'd picked up at the bakery on his way over and tossed a doughnut to the dog. The yeasty treat was gone in a second, and the pooch was licking its sugar-covered snout when Julia opened the front door.

"Oh, hi," she said, shifting the strap of her black bag higher onto her shoulder. "I was just heading off to work. But I'm glad I got to see you before I left. I wanted to thank you for…" Just then the hound walked over to its owner and sniffed Julia's hand.

"I think he's hoping for another treat," Kane explained when Julia seemed puzzled by her pet's response to her.

"A treat?"

"Yeah, Mr. Donut and I were just having a little manly breakfast out here before getting to work."

"Oh. Um, okay." Julia scrunched her nose as the dog wiggled its butt and waddled inside the house. Maybe she was one of those people who didn't give animals human food and didn't appreciate strangers taking liberties with their pets.

Kane wasn't taking a chance on making his work environment any more awkward than he'd already made it when he'd brought up the subject of dating and almost kissed his client. "I hope you don't mind."

"No. Of course not. You and Mr. Donut should eat whatever you like. But back to what I was saying. I wanted to thank you for returning to the store on Saturday and getting all that stuff for the house. I couldn't find a receipt, but let me know how much it all cost and I'll write you a check."

His throat constricted with annoyance at her money reference and he waved his hand. "We can settle up later."

She pursed her lips as if she was biting back an argument. Instead she said, "I'm so sorry I left you stranded at the hospital like that."

"No problem. Really. Don't even give it another thought." *Please*, Kane pleaded silently. *Let's not talk about that day anymore, or how I wanted to press you up against that display of seven-hundred-thread-count sheets and kiss you until you couldn't think of a single quality on your damn man list.*

To distract them both, he outlined his plans for what he hoped to get accomplished by this afternoon, and she nodded, stepping closer to him as her eyes followed the dog, which would occasionally walk by the open front door as he sniffed his way from room to room. Kane heard the lurch of a loud engine, and his sore arm brushed against Julia's soft sweater as they both turned to look at the delivery truck lumbering down the street.

He had no idea she'd been standing that close, and despite the sturdiness of his flannel shirt, Kane could feel the hair rise on his chest. It was all he could do not to think about the tingling sensation or the fact that he'd now accidentally touched her like that twice. Even he had to wonder how much of an accident it could be.

"I hate to run off like this, but do you think you can

show them where to put everything?" Her breath was warm and tinged with the lemon-lime smell of her morning beverage of choice. He could only imagine how sweet she would taste.

Focus, Chatterson.

He cracked his knuckles, then put his hands in his pockets before pulling them out and crossing his arms over his torso. "No problem."

When he heard the dog let out another growl toward the delivery men, Kane tossed him a second doughnut. *Attaboy.* At least he knew someone was protecting her.

"Okay, I guess I'm leaving you two in charge," Julia said, giving the hound another pat on his smooth head. Then she bolted toward her car and waved before driving off to the hospital.

"Well, big guy," Kane said to the pooch before walking down to help the men from Land O'Appliances unload. "Your mom didn't leave me any rules, so I guess she expects you to stay put and not get in my way today."

Yet all day long, the dog was close on his heels. Unlike its owner who couldn't seem to get away from Kane fast enough.

The sun was setting and Julia's stomach was already rumbling with hunger when she pulled into her driveway and saw the thickset basset hound sitting on her front porch. She sighed. It wasn't that Julia minded dogs. She just hadn't been around too many. In fact, she'd always wanted a pet of her own, but her father had been allergic to nearly anything with fur and four legs.

She supposed it might be kind of nice to have an animal around the house, and if Kane wanted to bring his dog to work with him, who was she to object? Especially after the guy had already gone above and beyond for her at the home goods store the other day.

Besides, Mr. Donut seemed relatively well-behaved enough, even if Julia did have some concerns about the healthiness of his diet. And the fact that the animal could probably benefit from a good scrubbing. But it wasn't any of her business—unless she found muddy paw prints on her new white comforter. She'd maybe have to say something to Kane at that point.

If she could get herself to stop sounding like a tongue-tied teenager in front of the man every time his heat-filled gaze turned in her direction. Speaking of which, why was he still working this late?

She set the parking brake and shoved the open box of chocolate-covered raisins back into her purse. When she walked in the door, she almost crashed into Kane's chest, making him drop his tool bag on the floor before he reached out a hand to steady her. And then her tongue twisted itself into a neat little knot again and a tingle shot from the base of her scalp to the back of her knees.

"Sorry. I meant to be gone by now," he said, and she tried not to notice the way the antique chandelier in the front parlor cast a fiery glow along the bronze stubble covering his jawline. "I was trying to get the kitchen sink installed before you got home. But when I heard you pull up, I threw in the towel and figured I'd get out of your hair for the night."

"You don't have to leave on my account." Although it probably would be better if he *and* his sexy five o'clock shadow left so that she could get back to avoiding all the sensations that got stirred up whenever he was near her.

"No, I need to leave on my own account. I'm going to drive myself crazy if I waste any more time on those antique pipes." He gestured toward the kitchen, and she saw the makeshift bandage on his thumb.

"You're hurt."

"What? This?" He shoved the injured digit, which appeared to be wrapped in a paper towel and duct tape, into his pocket. "Just busted my knuckle while I was trying to show that brushed nickel faucet who was boss. And lost."

"Oh no. Will the replica farm handle pump I picked out not work?"

"No, it'll work. But it's beyond my pay grade. I have a friend who specializes in plumbing, and I'm going to call him in to handle it for me. I hope you don't mind."

"Why would I mind?"

He shrugged his shoulders and did that chin wiping thing again. Which only drew her attention to his full mouth. "Some clients are funny about having subcontractors come into their houses without vetting them first."

"I'm not. I mean, I don't want just anybody working on my home, but I trust your judgment."

He gave her a questioning look and didn't respond. Julia couldn't tell if that meant *Of course you should trust my judgment* or *Why in the world would you trust my judgment*? Either way, she still had a lot to do tonight, and none of it would get done by standing in her entryway making small talk with the hard-to-read Kane Chatterson.

Her phone vibrated, and the screen indicated a new text message from Freckles. "Speaking of vetting people," Julia announced, glad for the excuse to look at something other than his chiseled face. "My aunt signed me up for one of those online dating sites today. She already filled out the application and paid the dues, but I need to log in there and change her answers and the profile she wrote for me before some romantic hopeful gets the wrong idea and messages me. It's going to be a long night cleaning up her potential mess."

"Online dating?" he asked, and she felt heat rise into her cheeks. *Now* he wanted to ask questions? He was supposed to take the hint and leave her alone to deal with her awkward social life. The one she didn't want.

"Embarrassing, right?"

"Not necessarily." He shrugged. "But how'd your aunt get you to agree to that? Never mind. I've met Freckles, and I've witnessed your negotiating skills."

The smallest hint of a grin danced along his lips, and suddenly Julia wanted to experience the full effect of Kane Chatterson's smile again. Even if it was at the expense of him teasing her. "You're never going to let me forget that trip to the appliance store, are you?"

"Not if you end up matched with a knucklehead like Paulie the Salesman, I won't."

"I would think I'm smart enough to have learned my lesson after dating one of my—" She cut herself off at the curious tilt of his head. Really, the fact that she'd foolishly been romantically involved with one of her charismatic college professors—before finding out he had a wife and a history of sleeping with most of his female TAs—was none of his business. Julia wasn't proud of the fact that her first, and only, intimate relationship had been built on her inability to see through Professor Mosely's lies. She didn't need Kane's curiosity or his pity, nor did she want to point out that she'd always had trouble with interpersonal skills. "Anyway, I promised Freckles that I would go out on three different dates to screen a candidate for my dreaded plus-one."

"With three different guys?" His tone made her think that three was too lofty an aspiration.

"I assume that's what she meant," Julia said, wishing

his eyebrows would stop lifting like that, mimicking her rising apprehension over what she'd agreed to.

"That's your problem, Jules. You see the world in black and white and you think everyone and every situation is going to go exactly by the book."

She crossed her arms and ignored the warm sensation that fluttered in her tummy at the nickname he'd now used twice. "They should. It makes more sense, logically, to take things at face value. It would be a lot easier to understand what people are thinking and fit in with them if we were all on the same page."

"It would be nice if it *were* that simple, but the real world doesn't work that way."

"I know." She sighed. In fact, nobody knew that better than her. "Which is why I'd rather go to the hospital fund-raiser alone. It's difficult enough feeling out of place at a social function with coworkers. Now I need to make sure I don't pick a date who is equally inexperienced and out of place."

Kane pulled his hands out of his pockets, used his bandaged thumb to click his gold watch open and closed a couple of times, then shoved the timepiece back in his pocket. Just when Julia thought she'd made him uncomfortable with all this dating talk, he said, "If you want, I could take a look at these guys before you decide to settle on the top three."

"Top three? I'd be lucky if I could find one who matched my list of requirements and wasn't old enough to be my grandfather."

"This would be your man list, right?" Kane asked, his eyebrows lifted.

Julia's cheeks couldn't get any hotter. Why had she allowed him to refinish the floorboards in the entryway? Now there was no chance of the glossy hardwood planks swallowing her up. "Please forget I ever mentioned that thing to you. Truly, it's not a serious list. And certainly not one that Aunt Freckles would likely follow."

"Let me take a look at it, and I'll help weed out the candidates that don't match. I'd hate to see you end up with some loser who wasn't good enough for you."

She'd been wrong about her cheeks. Flames of embarrassment rushed up Julia's neck and heated her entire face. There was absolutely no way she would ever show Kane Chatterson that pointless piece of paper where she'd written down what she was looking for in a man, especially since half the requirements were inspired by him.

"How do I know that you'd be any better at picking one?" She hoped that didn't come out too defensive, but she needed to get the subject off her list and her crummy dating life—or lack thereof.

"Because I have plenty of experience when it comes to this kind of thing."

He did? Curiosity was building inside her like a snowball rolling downhill, cooling her blush and causing her to forget all about professional boundaries. "So you date a lot?"

"I used… I mean, no. I don't date a lot, nor do I want to. But I'm the oldest of five kids, so I've got the protective older brother role down to a science."

And there was her answer. Disappointment threatened to crack her rib cage into a million pieces. Kane had never been interested in her that way. He was offering out of pity for her. Or brotherly concern. On the other hand, he might just want to make sure she didn't pick a sociopathic serial killer so that nothing happened to her or to the payment of his hefty remodeling fee. There was also the chance he just wanted a front-row seat to watching her fail epically at the one area she'd never been able to master in life—

Dating.

Sex.

Although, Julia had a feeling that sex with Kane Chatterson wouldn't feel like a failure at all.

Now where did that *thought come from?* she wondered.

She waved a dismissive hand and held open the front door. "I'll let you know if anything even comes of the process. Fingers crossed, nobody will even select me as a match and I'll be off the hook."

Kane's near-smile clamped into a tight line, and he bent to retrieve his tool bag off the floor. "Just make sure *you're* the one doing the selecting. Not the other way around."

"That's another lesson on negotiating. Got it."

"I'd better take off," he said, passing by her to get to the front door she'd left open. "Stay," he said to the hound thumping its tail against the battered planks of the front porch. Then he continued down the steps without his seemingly obedient canine.

Wait. Was he leaving his dog here?

"What about Mr. Donut?" she called out when he was climbing into his Bronco.

"What about him?" He slammed the heavy door closed, then rolled down the window.

"Doesn't he want to go with you?"

As though to answer for himself, the hound plopped down on his sizable belly—which wasn't too far off the ground, considering his short little legs—and rested his chin on Julia's foot.

"I don't know why he would," Kane said. "I'm all out of pastries. And to be honest with you, that old boy could probably benefit from one of those low-calorie brands of dog chow. I'm sure whatever you pick up at the feed store will be fine."

Julia tilted her head as he started up his engine. Was she missing something here? Had he sent her a text or an email about watching his dog for him, and she'd accidentally replied to it? She really needed to learn how to use that new cell phone.

"So, just to be clear," she called out over the sound of revving. "You want me to go buy him some diet dog food tonight?"

"That's up to you, but I think he's had plenty to eat already today, so you might as well grab it on your way home tomorrow. Also, I couldn't find a water bowl anywhere, so I just filled up one of the new baking dishes. I hope you don't mind."

Mind what? That he was using her brand-new bakeware to feed and water his dog? Well, to be honest, it wasn't like she was going to be cooking anything in it anytime soon—if ever. Or did she mind that in the space of five minutes, Kane Chatterson had implied that he thought of her as a sister and his personal pet-sitter?

She squatted down to stroke Mr. Donut's soft fur. He really was a sweet animal, and it might be kind of fun to play doggy owner for a day or so. It could be like a trial run of sorts to determine if she should get a pet of her own. Plus, it might be kind of nice not to be alone with her disillusionment tonight.

"I guess not," she said.

Kane's only acknowledgment was a small nod before driving off and leaving the basset hound happily drooling on her clogs.

"Come on, boy," she said, sliding her ugly but functional footwear out from under the dog's chin. His droopy brown eyes looked up at her as he followed her inside.

"I'm not sure where you're supposed to sleep, but it seems you've already made yourself at home. I sure wish your owner would've at least left me some instructions."

Maybe people in Sugar Falls did this sort of thing all the time. Perhaps she should be flattered that he trusted her with his pet. Julia had no idea if any of this was normal, but sometimes she got the feeling that her hired contractor wasn't normal, either. Which left her with another question.

Should she really be talking about her dating life with Kane Chatterson, let alone wishing he were a part of it?

Chapter Eight

"I knew I'd catch Legend Chatterson in here this morning," Kane heard Kylie Gregson say a week later as she gracefully sat down across from him and swiped a piece of his buttered rye toast.

He looked around to make sure there were only locals in the Cowgirl Up Café. The place might be decorated similar to the inside of Dolly Parton's horse stables, but it was also one of the few restaurants in town where he felt comfortable enough to let down his guard. "You know I hate it when people call me that, Kylie."

"Of course I know. But I'm your little sister. My job is to do stuff that you hate."

"Like volunteering me to hang out with your husband at his group therapy classes?" He took a sip of his decaf coffee.

"Please. You don't hate that, Kane. Just like you don't hate coming over for Thanksgiving dinner at my place."

He raised a questioning eyebrow at her before moving his plate out of her reach.

"That's why I stopped in this morning when I saw your old truck parked outside," his meddling sibling continued. "To make sure you're willing to run interference for me when Mom and Dad come to town next week."

"Have you suddenly learned how to cook?"

"No. But Luke and Carmen are bringing the boys, and she promised to help me in the kitchen. I figure we could do it potluck-style. So what will you be bringing?"

"If Dad doesn't promise to behave, some antacid and an excuse to leave early."

"You know what, Kane Chatterson? Because I'm your sister and I think our father has been too soft on you lately, I'm going to tell you straight up what everyone else has been too afraid to say. Ever since you've stopped playing baseball and exiled yourself to Sugar Falls, you're no fun anymore."

"Says the new mom of twin babies." He redistributed some of the sausage gravy onto his hash browns. His sister was worse than his agent, Charlie, who Kane really needed to bite the bullet and fire once and for all. But he didn't even like to think about his former career, let alone talk about it out loud. In a public place. "Where are my nieces, anyway? I'm surprised you could get away this long."

"Drew has them this morning. I have a lot of work at the office I need to catch up on, and he wanted me to stop in and see you because you can't refuse the invitation in person."

"Fine. I'll come to your Thanksgiving dinner, and I'll even bring something."

"Perfect. I already put you in charge of beer and wine."

"That's about all I'm capable of these days." In fact,

a few years ago, nobody would've put Kane Chatterson in any position of responsibility. So at least he was improving.

"Not from what I hear." Kylie's singsong voice rattled around his head, just like she'd probably intended for it to do.

"You of all people should know better than to listen to gossip."

"Oh please. I'm a psychologist's wife with two kids under nine months and a full-time accounting practice. Unless Drew has an afternoon off and we manage to luck out by getting both girls down for a nap at the same time, small-town gossip is the only entertainment I've got left."

"Ew."

"Anyway, I heard you've gotten a lot done over at the Pinecone Court house."

He grunted and then shoved the plate of toast in Kylie's direction when it became evident that she wasn't going to leave him in peace anytime soon.

"How's the new boss lady?" his sister asked breezily, as if he didn't know exactly which direction she was headed with this.

He grunted again, wishing the beard he'd shaved several months ago was still there to hide the heat rising in his cheeks. It had been a couple of days since he'd called in the plumber to finish her kitchen, and with the roofing company he'd subcontracted at her place every day trying to lay new shingles before the typical late November snowstorms, he and Julia hadn't had any more awkward moments alone where they talked about dating and one of them ended up high-tailing it to their car before they did something they'd regret. As much as he wanted to see her again, it was a good thing he'd been making an effort to avoid her because it forced him to focus on the house remodel and not on the woman who hurled his common sense into the off-season.

"Drew said he ran into you guys in Boise not too long ago and she seemed friendly."

Another grunt.

"I hear she's a hotshot brain surgeon over at Shadowview. Doesn't seem like the kind of woman you normally go for." Kylie, along with the rest of his family, knew how to rattle him into giving them even a small sliver of information. And he felt his tight-lipped determination slowly slipping.

"Who said I was going for anybody?" Kane asked after swallowing a bite of scrambled eggs. Not in a burrito this time, though, as he'd learned that he preferred his breakfast in plain sight.

"You want a menu, Kylie?" Freckles asked before setting down a glass of orange juice in front of his sister. The café owner's question was rhetorical since menus were usually used only by the tourists who filled up the place on weekends.

"No, thanks. I think I'll have a ham biscuit. To go, please. I can't remember the last time I actually had time to sit down and eat a real meal."

"Babies and jobs will do that to a woman." Freckles winked. "Speaking of jobs, Kane, has my niece been getting home from work at a reasonable hour?"

He kept his eyes locked onto the plate of food before him, not wanting to witness his sister's ears physically perk up at that information the way Mr. Donut's floppy ones lifted whenever a delivery truck rolled down the street. "I wouldn't know, ma'am. I'm usually gone by the time she gets there."

"That's what I was afraid of," Freckles said, leaning

against the side of their booth. Now both Kane's and Kylie's ears were at full attention.

"Why's that?" Kylie asked Freckles, and he was thankful he'd be able to get more information without having to be the one to get his gossip-free hands dirty.

"She works crazy hours and has absolutely no social life. It ain't normal, I tell you." Freckles shook her head.

Kane glanced at the woman's neon-green sneakers, snakeskin leather pants and fuchsia polka-dot suspenders. Freckles really wasn't the best one to be defining *normal*.

"Is she happy, though?" Kylie asked before taking a drink of orange juice and settling back in her seat. Since the chatty waitress hadn't put in her order yet, nobody was going anywhere for a while. At least, that's what Kane told himself to alleviate his guilt at sitting here like some nosy busybody instead of asking for his check and hauling butt out the doors painted to look like the entrance to a saloon.

"I can't really tell," the older woman said, then put her hand on her hip. "What do you think, Kane? You probably see her more than me. You think Julia's happy?"

He scrunched his nose, not wanting to be a part of this conversation at all. "How should I know? I barely talk to her."

"See?" Freckles said. "The girl doesn't talk much to anyone. Probably because her parents were big on that whole 'children should be seen and not heard' child-rearing method. I tried not to be too opinionated since I rarely made it out there except for the occasional holiday, telling myself that they were doing what they thought was best, pushing her to excel all the time. But kids need to play, to have fun. And they were just so structured with her. Not that Julia knew any better. I just wish my sweet little niece knew how to cut loose now and then."

Kane thought of Julia's regularly unmade bed and the dishes she'd left in the sink each morning after heading for work. Apparently her housekeeping skills were something she'd decided to cut loose on. But mentioning that seemingly personal tidbit of information to her aunt, who ran a tight ship in her kitchen, would be somewhat of a betrayal to his client. Plus, he liked holding on to a bit of knowledge about Dr. Smarty-Pants that no one else was privy to. Oh, the secrets one discovered when given unrestricted access to another person's house.

"It sounds like we need to get her out more," Kylie said, and Kane recognized the mischievous glint in his sister's eye.

"Not everyone is a party girl like you, Kylie," Kane grumbled, more to himself than anything, because he could see Freckles quickly warning up to the irresponsible suggestion.

"That's what I've been telling her." The waitress wagged a long purple-painted fingernail in the air. "I even signed her up for an online dating website."

"Any success with that?" Kylie leaned forward. He had to wonder if these women realized they were trying to manage Julia's life as much as her parents once had. Only in the opposite direction.

"Just between me, you and the fence post..." Freckles looked around, and Kane decided that Scooter and Jonesy, the two old cowboys sitting at their usual booth and blatantly listening in to the conversation, must be the fence posts. "She met a man for coffee two days ago and said he was nice enough. But since I set up her account, I have the password and decided to go onto the website and do a little snooping. I looked the guy up and found out that he had no job and claimed to be in what he called an 'open relationship.'" Freckles used her fingers to add air quotes to the last part.

Kane found his fingers clenching again. She was supposed to be a doctor. A genius. Didn't the woman know how to screen these guys? This was why he'd offered to help her meet someone in the first place. Julia didn't know a blasted thing about men or how they thought. At the rate she was going, best case scenario was that she'd get matched with some sleazy dirtbag who would embarrass her at the hospital fund-raiser.

Worst case scenario, she was setting herself up for someone to take advantage of her. The woman's heart was as big as the third-story turret on her home. She was prime pickings for some gold-digging, power-hungry loser who would come into her life and start changing things around. Like putting in a tacky man cave where the formal library should be, or wanting to knock down the gabled roofline to install a satellite dish. Or sending Mr. Donut off to doggy reform school—which, frankly, wouldn't be a bad thing since the pooch had been sneaking into Kane's tool bag whenever it was unattended and, so far, had ferreted out a crescent wrench, two Phillips screwdrivers and a tape measure. He'd even blamed the basset hound for eating one of the paintbrushes he'd been using to stain the balustrade along the second floor and had been about to rush the poor, senseless animal to the emergency vet in town. But then Kane realized he'd accidentally left the brush on top of the stepladder when he'd gotten a phone call from one of the guys in Drew's therapy group.

Which was why Kane now went through Julia's house every morning after she'd left, making sure she hadn't left any food or other dangerous items sitting out where the dog could get them. Besides, Kane needed an organized workspace. He didn't do well with messes or distractions.

He was in his own world, having no idea how he'd wandered down the mental road from Julia's asinine online dating plan to his missing tools, when he overheard his sister say to Freckles, "I have a great idea. Why don't you and your niece come for Thanksgiving dinner?"

Wait. What Thanksgiving dinner? The one Kylie had just roped *him* into attending? The one his sister had said she needed him at to run interference on his domineering parents? Well, just their father, really. Mom always took a backseat to his old man's crazy schemes.

But before Kane could suggest that subjecting anyone to the overbearing presence known as Bobby Chatterson would swear poor Julia off social gatherings forever, the older woman gave Kylie a grateful smile. "We'd love to, hon. Thanks for the invite."

"I'll ask Drew and Luke to invite one of their single Navy friends. There's bound to be someone we can set her up with."

"You'd do that for her?" Freckles's heavily lashed eyes opened wide.

"Of course. If you promise to bring a few dozen of your famous buttermilk biscuits for dinner. Maybe a dessert or two?"

"You're on," the waitress said, five inches of jangling silver bracelets clinking together when she stuck out her hand to shake on the deal.

The sound reminded Kane of what shackled prisoners must have heard as they were being marched to their execution.

"Are you sure I'm not underdressed?" Julia asked her aunt when they drove up and parked in the circular drive of the Gregsons' lakefront house.

"You look beautiful, Sug." Aunt Freckles reached over

and patted the knee of her niece's black tailored slacks, which were expensive and well cut, but also very understated.

When Julia was growing up, formal dinners meant long, elegant dresses and heirloom pieces of jewelry from the built-in safe in her mother's dressing room. However, judging by her aunt's choice of a brown leather miniskirt and tall moccasin boots, the people of Sugar Falls celebrated the holidays a bit more casually. Freckles's orange sweater with the words Gobble Gobble stitched on the front was a far cry from any of the fancy clothes in Julia's own sparse closet.

"Now help me get these biscuits inside. I hear Kylie and Drew had Kane install one of those fancy double ovens in the kitchen, so I hope she won't mind me popping them in to bake before dinner. We can come back for all the pies."

Kane? Would he be here? Julia's hand trembled slightly as she reached for the passenger door handle. Certainly Drew wouldn't invite one of his patients for dinner. Not that Julia knew how they did things in smaller towns, but she couldn't imagine her mother ever entertaining her own patients.

She looked around at the other cars in the driveway and didn't spot his Bronco anywhere. Maybe she should've made more inquiries ahead of time. Not that she minded seeing him. But she hadn't had an actual conversation with the man in almost a week. Just notes in passing about built-in bookcases for the den or the delivery of the mahogany armoire she'd bought at an antiques shop in downtown Sugar Falls.

After the way her body had been responding to him lately, she hadn't even trusted herself to speak to him on the telephone. Which was maybe an overreaction on her part, because there were quite a few things she needed to speak to him about—like the way he assumed she wouldn't mind taking care of his pet.

She'd made the mistake of leaving a note for him regarding the low-calorie dog food she'd picked up for Mr. Donut, and Kane had apparently taken that as an invitation to leave his dog there overnight indefinitely. Then she'd come home from a grueling eighteen-hour day last Wednesday to find that he'd also taken the liberty of bringing over some fancy stuffed pillow for the basset hound to sleep on. Perhaps she should've told him that his pet didn't bother with the bed at all when it seemed more comfortable using her air mattress.

She exited the car and walked toward the rear of Freckles's turquoise Ford Flex, still brooding about the dog. It wasn't like she could blame Mr. Donut. The bedding Kane had picked out for her temporary bed was very plush and luxurious, even if she had learned the hard way to check under the down comforter for various tools that the animal liked to hide there.

"So, who else is coming for dinner?" Julia whispered to her aunt as she balanced a tray in one hand and straightened her necklace with the other. The pearls had been in her family for generations and, besides her mom's watch, was the only piece of jewelry she'd brought with her when she'd moved to Idaho. It was also the only thing she had to liven up the pale gray cashmere sweater she'd opted for rather than accepting her aunt's offer to buy them matching turkey-themed tops.

"Just the Gregsons and the Chattersons," Freckles replied before an oversize teak door opened and a boy with curly blond hair launched out of it.

"Did you bring the chocolate pie, Miss Freckles?"

Wait. Did she just say the Chattersons?

As in, her moody contractor?

Before Julia could question whether she was seeing double, a duplicate boy darted out.

"What other kinds of pies did you bring?" The other boy asked. In less than a second, two bouncing blond heads were on either side of her and peeking into the rear hatch. "You want us to help you carry stuff, Miss Freckles?"

The older woman, who could match anyone in energy, didn't miss a beat. "Yes. And yes. Sug, allow me to introduce Aiden and Caden Gregson, two of the finest dessert connoisseurs the town of Sugar Falls has ever seen." Her aunt patted each twin's head as she said his name, but Julia had no idea how anyone could tell them apart. "Boys, I'd like you to meet my niece, Dr. Julia Fitzgerald."

"Our Uncle Drew is a doctor," one of the boys said. "But he's just the talking kind. He doesn't even have those plastic gloves in his office, so he can't make cool balloon hands or nothing. What kinda doctor are you?"

"Okay, monkeys," Drew Gregson called from the front porch, his arm wrapped around the waist of a tall redheaded woman. "Let's allow our guests to come inside the house before you ask them a million questions."

The boys ran back and forth as the striking couple made their way to their car.

"Hi, I'm Kylie Gregson," Drew's wife said, her smile and handshake almost as exuberant as the constantly moving twins. "We're so glad you could join us for Thanksgiving, Dr. Fitzgerald."

"Please, call me Julia," she started, but before she could thank her hosts for their invitation, her voice trailed off as her eyes were drawn back to the front of the house where a hatless, clean-shaven Kane Chatterson stood.

He was here. And he was dressed up. Her vocabulary went on sabbatical and her muscles felt about as firm as the yeasty circles of raw biscuit dough lining the baking sheet she was trying not to drop.

"Is *Fitzgerald* one word or two words?" Caden—or was it Aiden?—asked as he grabbed Julia's hand, breaking her out of the frozen trance she'd fallen into the moment Kane had appeared on the front porch. "Because when Carmen marries my dad, her new name is going to be two words. But we won't have to call her Officer Delgado Gregson on account of she'll be our mom."

Julia blinked several times. Who were these kids and what in the world were they talking about? If her overwhelmed head hadn't been spinning at their rapid-fire sentences, she might have been tempted to command her unsteady body to retreat inside Freckles's car and get her pulse under control. Julia wasn't used to children, and she especially wasn't accustomed to ones who were so welcoming and friendly. Kane smiled at her as he grabbed the tray of biscuits from the hand not enclosed in the smaller, damper one of Aiden or Caden Gregson.

"Welcome to crazy town," he said low enough for only her to hear. "You want to come inside and meet the rest of the circus?"

Her heart fluttered up into her throat and all she could manage was a nod. The proximity of his voice, coupled with his rare smile, was enough to make her agree to jump into a cage of dancing lions with him if that's what he'd asked.

"Miss Freckles brought a ton of dessert, Uncle Kane," one of the twins said as they led the procession of baked goods up the front steps. "Which means we can have that pie-eating contest, after all."

Uncle Kane? He was related to these people? The assumption that he was Drew's patient, along with every other preconceived notion she'd made about the man was suddenly replaced by an empty void, leaving her anxious to figure out the answers to refill it.

"I hope you boys know better than to challenge your Uncle Kane to *any* kind of contest," said a man who looked exactly like Drew Gregson, minus the glasses. "They don't call him 'the Legend' for nothing." He turned to Julia and grinned. "Hi, I'm Luke and these little pie-eating chatterboxes are mine."

The name Legend would imply that Kane was legendary at something. Unless it was for his ability to go hours without saying a single word or ever mentioning the fact that he had family living nearby, Julia couldn't imagine what kind of contest Kane might win. Instead of asking for clarification, though, she shook hands with the boys' father, and then with more people once she was ushered inside.

Drew and Kylie's Craftsman-style home boasted an open floor plan with a long counter separating the great room from the elaborate kitchen, making it easy for the guests to interact with each other over the chaos of pots and pans. A pair of matching pink baby swings swaying out of sync, the blaring television and some sort of board game were set up in front of it.

Julia had never been more thankful for her uncanny ability to remember names and faces, because there were a lot of twins in this extended family. And somehow, Kane was related to them all.

Luke, a Navy recruiter and Drew's twin brother, introduced her to his fiancée, Carmen, an officer with the Sugar Falls Police Department.

The connection that surprised her most was that Kane and Kylie were siblings. Although now that she finally saw Kane without his usual hat, the physical resemblance between the vivacious mom and the quiet contractor was apparent as they both got their hair color from their father.

Bobby Chatterson was a bear of a man and kept young Aiden and Caden engaged in what appeared to be a high-stakes game of *Battleship*. From what Julia could tell, the man wasn't technically their grandfather, but the boys lovingly called him Coach, and he would launch a full tickle attack when he caught one of them sneaking looks at the coordinates of his small plastic submarine and destroyer.

As soon as Mr. Chatterson found out that Julia was not only in the Navy but also an officer he was quick to enlist her as his teammate against the two adorable but sneaky opponents.

"Are you sure I shouldn't be helping cook or something?" Julia asked when Freckles and Carmen joined Lacey Chatterson, Kane's mom, near the double oven.

"Nah." Kane's dad waved a thick, freckled hand as if he were swatting a fly. "Drew already did most of the cooking, anyway. Lacey and Carmen are just hiding out in there because these two little hustlers here beat them double or nothing, and nobody else is willing to give these young pups a real run for their money. I need a teammate with a solid background in military subterfuge."

"And I don't have a solid military background, Coach?" Luke said from across the room. "You *do* know that I was team leader of my SEAL unit, and I'm currently the commanding officer of recruiting for the Western Idaho district, right?"

Bobby Chatterson rolled his eyes. "We've been over this, Luke. I don't care how many push-ups you can do or how many airplanes you've jumped out of. Your poker face is a worse giveaway than that nervous tic of Kane's when he rubs his chin. The boys can read a play from you two from a mile away. So what do you say, Captain? We allies or what?"

Julia looked at the older Gregson twins, her fellow Navy brethren who were probably much better equipped to handle an intense strategist like Kane's father, yet seemed equally reluctant to do so. "I've never played *Battleship*," she began. "Besides, I'm mostly trained for what happens inside the infirmary, not for complete naval warfare."

"Good point," Mr. Chatterson said, then turned to his daughter, who was nursing one of the babies. "Hey, Kylie, do you guys have that game *Operation*? Julia's on my team."

"Sorry, Dad. We just have that one and chess."

"Yeah, figures your shrink of a husband would only prefer the head games."

Julia sucked in a startled gasp at the insult, but the rest of the adults laughed.

"You're just jealous that you've been on a sound losing streak since your granddaughters were born," Drew shot back at his father-in-law.

"I have a feeling my luck's about to change with this one." Mr. Chatterson used a tree-branch-size thumb to gesture in her direction.

"Dad, leave Julia alone." Kane spoke from behind the U-shaped sofa. "If she doesn't want to play a board game with you guys, she doesn't have to."

Julia squared her shoulders, not needing Kane to protect her. She wanted to fit in with this fun-loving and quick-bantering family. "I'd be honored to be your teammate," she said, sitting on the plush wool rug beside the older man and folding her legs under the dark pine coffee table, which served as the command post.

Apparently Julia was in fact good luck for Mr. Chatterson, as they won the next two games against the Gregson boys, who were surprisingly cutthroat in their precision and execution of moves. She knew her upbringing had been unique, but how many families got to sit around playing games and watching football on television during the holidays? Maybe it was routine for the Chatterson gang, but this was a first for her.

When the kids ran off to play outside, Julia stayed where she was, comfortable but out of the way. Kane had stopped pacing long enough to sit on the sofa behind her. She could feel his restless leg brush against her back every time one of the sportscasters on television made a reference to some exclusive baseball interview coming up after the game. While the occasional contact was seemingly inadvertent on his part, Julia found herself leaning back slightly to put pressure against his jostling knee, which would cause him to pause, even if only momentarily.

She was well-versed in neurobehavioral disorders as well as neurological matters, and it wasn't the first time she'd suspected that Kane Chatterson's many nervous gestures and his inability to sit still or stay focused were ongoing issues for him. But because he never talked about himself—or about anything, really—she didn't want to diagnose him so readily.

What she *wasn't* well-versed in, however, was family dynamics. Despite the easy camaraderie between the seemingly tight-knit group, Julia immediately sensed that there was something about Bobby Chatterson that had his son on edge. Of course, Kane often seemed on edge to her anyway, so maybe she was overthinking things.

But while all the other men seemed comfortable teasing each other and talking about people Julia didn't really know, the elder Chatterson kept giving his son pointed looks, and the knee behind her back would spring into action again and again.

Trying to solve the riddle kept Julia's brain from contemplating her physical reaction to Kane's continued closeness and accidental touch. But no matter how much she was conditioned to think logically, she was having difficulty commanding her body to remain neutral. Being this close to him alternated between a pleasant fluttering feeling in her lower extremities and involuntarily being stuck in one of those vibrating massage chairs at the mall.

"Here," Bobby Chatterson said to Kylie when one of the babies started crying. "Let me take her."

"Thanks, Dad," Kylie said. "Carmen said dinner's ready, so let's make our way to the dining room."

After a minor argument between the boys over whose turn it was to sit by Coach and three rounds of rock-paper-scissors, Carmen and Luke put one son on each side of the patriarch and newly crowned *Battleship* champ.

"Divide and conquer," Carmen whispered to her, and Julia was again flattered that this group had welcomed her so willingly into their personal lives.

The large family sat down at the even larger table, which was decorated just as stunningly as the rest of the house. They might have openly teased Kylie about not being a good cook, but Julia had to admit that Kane's sister was at the top of her class when it came to decorating skills. In fact, Julia was tempted to ask for the new mom's input when it came time to furnish her own house.

She'd gathered that the Gregsons had just moved here after renting out Kylie's much smaller condo. The sizable home was done mostly in neutrals of beige and stone with strategically placed green shades throughout to liven things up. The food was perfect, and the wine flowed along with lighthearted conversation and slightly competitive banter. Kane even made a couple of jokes about his father, who apparently had recently added some poundage to what was already a thick frame.

Kane had taken the seat next to Julia and passed her only the dishes that he knew were vegetarian-friendly. She was touched by his consideration and the fact that nobody had treated her like an outsider for eating differently.

"So, you still happy living out here in Idaho and just being a contractor?" Bobby Chatterson asked his son, and Julia looked around the room to see if she was the only one who'd heard the emphasis on the word *just*.

Kane leaned behind her back to send the gravy boat to Luke. "As happy as I could expect."

That was an odd answer, but Bobby simply nodded before reaching across one of the boys to fork a piece of white meat onto Lacey's plate, then taking a few slices of turkey for himself. Julia noticed that with each dish coming his way, the man served his wife first—just like his son was doing for her. She shifted in her seat, not wanting to dwell on the similarity.

Kane's dad stared across the table at him. "You know what I want to say, right?"

Apparently the entire table—including the nine-month-old girls, who both looked up from the mashed potatoes and peas they were exchanging across their high chair trays—knew what the elder Chatterson wanted to say. Julia took a sip of her wine, wishing she could be clued in.

"Yes, Dad. We talk about wasting talents and meeting

my potential every time you call me. You aren't telling me anything new."

"Then I won't push you, son."

"You won't push me?" Kane asked, his eyes narrowing. "What's the catch?"

"No catch. I just want my kids happy. Even you, sourpuss."

"But...?" Kane took a sip of his pale ale. Julia's calf muscles clenched, reminding her she was practically sitting on the edge of her chair.

"But your mom would like to know when you're going to settle down and give us some more grandkids."

Julia heard several snorts, along with a chorus of snickering coming from the end of the table near Luke Gregson and her own Aunt Freckles.

"Bobby Chatterson, don't you go putting words in my mouth," Lacey said before spearing a bite of green beans her husband had just spooned onto her plate.

"Okay, so *I'd* like to know when you're giving us some more grandkids. Your mom's not getting any younger, you know."

Mrs. Chatterson responded with a sharp elbow to her husband's rib cage. Either Aiden or Caden asked if this time they could have a boy cousin.

"I don't know, Dad." Kane replied, shrugging one shoulder as if he didn't intend to give the subject any thought. "Why don't you ask Kaleb when *he* plans to settle down and give you grandkids?"

"Oh, you know your brother Kaleb. I think he relishes being the black sheep of the family. He marches to the beat of his own drum, that one."

"If by that you mean he runs a successful multimillion dollar gaming company, then beat away," Drew said. "Actually, Julia, you'd probably like Kaleb. He's very intelligent, very well-read. Do you know if he's dating anyone right now, Kane?"

"How the hell should I know?" Kane took another drink and, seeing the tablecloth rustling, she could only imagine the way his knee was bouncing beneath it. "I'm the only one in this family who seems to mind his own business."

"Last time I talked to him, he wasn't seeing anyone special," Kylie said. "When he comes out for Christmas, we should introduce him to Julia."

Julia gulped, then gave a noncommittal murmur, unsure of what her response should be. Were they trying to set her up with Kane's brother? Or were they just being polite and trying to include her in the conversation? These were the kinds of social intricacies she wished she could better navigate.

She remembered auditioning for the District of Columbia's youth chamber orchestra when she'd been nine years old. She'd practiced the Vivaldi concerto on her cello for hours a day and knew the piece forward and backward. But when she'd gotten on stage, her mother had told the conductor Julia would be performing the Tchaikovsky instead. Later, her mom had explained that it was important for her to learn to be adaptable and to overcome her insecurities, despite being so unprepared.

Sitting around this table reminded Julia of that experience. She had the feeling there was a performance going on, but she'd practiced for one situation and was thrown into another, one she was utterly unprepared for.

"You know who else we should introduce to Julia?" Luke Gregson said, his fork poised in the air as if he was about to start a PowerPoint presentation of eligible bachelors. Julia's stomach dropped when everyone's eyes turned his way. "My buddy, Renault. He was on the

SEAL team with me and just moved to the area a few months ago, too. He's supposed to stop by later tonight, after he gets done serving dinner at the homeless veterans' shelter."

"You guys are making Julia uncomfortable with all your matchmaking talk," Kane said. She suddenly realized she was sunk down so low in her seat, her chest was inches away from the marshmallow-covered sweet potatoes on her plate.

"Sorry, Captain," Bobby Chatterson said. "I only meant to steer my boy into the right direction. We didn't mean to bring your single status into any of this."

"Well, Dad," Kane said defensively, "you shouldn't be trying to steer anyone."

Looking down the table at Aunt Freckles, who was on her third glass of cabernet sauvignon—not counting what she might or might not have consumed in the kitchen before the meal started—Julia saw her aunt following the conversation as though she were watching a match at Wimbledon.

"I don't know, Lace." Bobby finally said to his wife. "It seems like no matter how hard we try to plan out their lives for them, these kids of ours have their own minds."

Julia knew firsthand what it was like to have parents pushing you into their idea of perfection. Luckily she'd been able to meet their expectations. But she could practically feel the annoyance in Kane's tense leg beside her. She wondered if he felt like the failure in the family compared to his recently married CPA sister and an apparently wealthy younger brother. While none of them had come out and criticized Kane directly, the stirring need to defend him and his life choices caused her to speak up.

"Kane is doing a fabulous job remodeling my house," she said, then wondered if her off-the-cuff pronouncement sounded more like an unexpected toast. "He is extremely skilled and dedicated. Personally, I don't think he's wasting his talents at all."

Nobody made a sound. and Julia felt the weight of everyone's stares—minus that of one of the babies, who'd fallen asleep with homemade applesauce smeared all over her tiny face. But the only gaze she met was Kane's. His entire body had shifted so he was facing her, his head tilted to the side as if to ask her to repeat what she'd just said.

"Hey, guys," Caden said, interrupting the awkward silence. "Now that we're all done with dinner, who wants to try out the new double bike Uncle Drew bought us?"

"Uncle Drew is going to get payback for that little gift," Luke Gregson vowed, and the unexplainable tension shifted just like that, returning the conversation back to a playful banter.

"That's the same thing you said when Uncle Kane bought us that bow-and-arrow set for our birthday," Aiden said.

She looked at Kane and saw his face slowly relax into a smirk. A bow-and-arrow set for nine-year-olds? Maybe his family was right to question the man's ability to make good decisions.

"Good point," Luke said, one arm around Carmen's shoulders. "I'm sure Uncle Kane would like to try out the new tandem bike."

"What about you, Dr. Julia?" Caden asked. "You wanna take a turn with Uncle Kane?"

"Oh, I don't know. I've never ridden a bike before."

"Never?" Aiden asked. "Like ever?"

"Well, I've used a stationary one at the gym," she clarified as she squared her shoulders, not willing to admit to the table, or to herself, that she couldn't do something. "I can't imagine it'd be much different to ride yours."

"It's way different." Kane shook his head. "This one actually requires balance."

"I can balance," she said. She'd practically balanced on the edge of her seat throughout the entire meal.

"You're saying you could just hop on a bike and start riding it, no problem?" Kane rested his arm on the back of her chair, his chest appearing to be a bit more puffed out than usual—as though he were throwing out a challenge.

"If I wanted to, I could," she said, almost convincing herself.

"It's not that hard," Bobby Chatterson said. "I've taught my share of kids, and you look like a sturdy enough gal to me." Julia wasn't sure, but she thought that coming from the opinionated man who resembled a lumberjack himself, it was meant as a compliment.

"I don't know, Sug." Aunt Freckles suddenly took a break from sipping her wine to speak up. "If you take a nasty fall, you'll end up in a cast right before the Sugar and Shadow Shindig. Think of how that would look in the evening dress you just ordered."

"I'm not going to break a limb," Julia said, rolling her eyes. "How hard can it be to hold on to the handlebar and pedal at the same time?"

"Okay then," Kane said, his smooth chin lifted in such a way that he had to look down his nose at her even though they were sitting side by side. "Let's go outside and you can prove it."

She didn't want to prove anything. At least, not in front of witnesses. She looked at the ceiling, wondering how she was going to get herself and her pride out of this situation. "I should probably stay here and help clean up the kitchen."

"So you can't do it?" The corner of Kane's mouth was tilted up.

"Kane, last week I used a robotic arm to conduct a laser ablation of a deep-seated tumor on a patient's brain. I think I can manage a bicycle," Julia said.

"Care to make a wager?" he asked, and Lacey Chatterson looked to the ceiling while her husband smacked his palms together.

Oh boy. Betting was another thing Julia had never done. But she wasn't about to confess that to this group. "What kind of wager?"

"Ooh, I know," Aiden—or was it Caden?—said. "Whoever loses has to do something embarrassing, like dress up in a pig costume and do a funny dance in the gazebo at Town Square Park."

"Where are we going to get a pig outfit on Thanksgiving?" his nine-year-old brother responded. "A turkey one would probably be easier to find."

While Freckles and Kylie chimed in with suggestions about available costumes, Julia looked at Kane and knew exactly what she wanted if she won the bet. "If I prove that I can ride the bike, then you have to go to the Sugar and Shadow Shindig."

"What about the plus-one?" Kane asked.

"You can bring a date if you want. It's up to you."

"No, I meant what about *your* plus-one?"

"I don't know who that is yet, remember?"

He slowly smiled. "That's right. Which means, if you can't ride the bike, *I* get to choose your date."

Chapter Nine

Kane wished he'd never challenged Julia to learn how to ride this blasted tandem bicycle. Then, to make matters worse, he'd popped off and issued the most idiotic wager in the history of all idiotic wagers. If she won, he'd be stuck attending the stupid hospital fund-raiser dance next month. If he won, he would have to sit home alone and wonder about whomever he ended up picking as Julia's date and whether the jerk was treating her well and keeping his hands to himself.

It was a lose-lose situation.

"Stop leaning to the left," he called out behind him. "You're going to make us fall over."

"But the boys said I need to lean left when I want to go right."

"Jules, you're the stoker. I'm the captain."

"So?"

"So, when you're the person in back, you can go only where the person in front steers you."

"Maybe I should try being in the front," she suggested. "That way, I can steer."

"For the eighteenth time, until you can learn how to hold yourself upright, I'm not letting you near the front seat."

"Has anyone ever told you that you have control issues, Kane Chatterson?"

That was an understatement if ever there was one.

As they pedaled clumsily around the driveway, Kane's thoughts kept turning to the idea of Julia...dating. And how distasteful the idea was. He'd be damned if he'd let his family set Just Julia up with his brainiac younger brother Kaleb. Or, for that matter, Luke's macho navy SEAL friend, Renault. The guy sounded like a total loser, if you asked Kane, and not at all the type of man Julia should be interested in. What kind of name was Renault anyway?

He'd almost volunteered to go as her date himself, but knew better than to set himself up for rejection with his family there to make fun of him. Plus, her suggestion that he bring his own plus-one was all the evidence he needed that she'd rather give someone the Heimlich maneuver again than go to a social function with him. So now he was stuck trying to teach her how to ride this stupid tandem bike, completely unsure of whether he wanted her to succeed or fail.

All he knew was that if she didn't start maintaining some sense of balance, he was going to fall and break his other shoulder and wind up doubly screwed—with all of his family witnessing the potential crash.

"Hmph," he said as he overcorrected to the right. "Now that you've met my family, you can see that I came by my control issues naturally."

"That's definitely a fair assessment." He heard her

chuckle from behind him. "Hey, did it bother you when your dad was asking you all those questions about your future?"

Julia was more likely to pedal while she talked, and the only way to remain upright was to keep her pedaling in sync with him. Which meant he had to keep her distracted with conversation.

"Not really," he admitted. "I know they all worry about me, but I guess I've given them plenty of reason to in the past."

"Why would they worry? Because they don't think you're meeting your true potential?"

"That and the fact that I went through a lot these past two years."

"Any chance you want to tell me about it?" she asked.

They'd successfully made it around the driveway twice, and Kane wanted to venture onto the asphalt road now that their audience was slowly trickling into the warmth of the house, taking Julia's discarded coat inside with them.

"Not while I'm trying to keep us from falling on our faces."

"I think I know what your problem is," Julia said, and he felt the pace of the pedals pick up tempo, along with his heart rate.

"Trust me, I'm dealing with more than just one hang-up."

"You're afraid to fail." He heard the smugness in her voice and didn't want her thinking she was right. Or worse—him to start believing it.

"And you're not?" he asked.

"I'm not afraid of it, no. I simply refuse to."

"Have you ever failed at anything?"

He felt the bike jerk ever so slightly and wondered if his question had surprised Dr. Smarty-Pants. He knew from past experience, both on the mound and from participating in Drew's group therapy, that now was the time to push for an answer. "C'mon, Jules. You can tell me."

"I think it's no secret that I don't do so well at personal relationships." He could barely hear her admission as a minivan whizzed by them along the neighborhood street.

"Yeah, I don't know how you define *personal relationships*, but you handled yourself just fine back there with my spectacle of a family, including my old man."

"That's different. That's simply blending in and keeping a low profile. Besides, your dad was grateful that I saved his patrol boat from being blasted out of the water on that last round of *Battleship*."

Kane wasn't one for pep talks, receiving them or giving them. But he had a feeling there was more to this failure story of hers, and the only way he was going to hear it was if he assured her that he was on her team. "Plus," he continued, "you've managed to make it through the ranks as a naval officer. I doubt you could do that if you had some serious personality flaws."

"Actually, all I have to do is be a good doctor and follow orders. So the Navy has been pretty easy for me."

"Then help me figure this out. What kind of relationships are you talking about?"

"You know," she said, and he could almost hear her blush. "The one-on-one kind."

"Like with friends?"

"Well, that and..." Her voice trailed off.

Kane pulled off the road. They'd gone at least a mile by now and were almost at Snowflake Boulevard. Although Julia was finally able to maintain a steadier pace and they'd had only one near miss when they'd had to swerve around a raccoon darting past them, he definitely didn't want to tempt fate by steering them into a higher traffic area. Plus, he wanted to look at her. He planted his feet on the ground and pivoted his torso around.

"That and what? Dating?"

"Yes, dating." Her head slumped forward, and her whole body probably would have followed suit if she hadn't had to stand on tiptoe to balance on the still bike.

He wasn't sure if the rosiness on her cheeks was from exertion or from embarrassment at him blurting out something she wasn't an expert at. Remembering the vision of her in her spandex workout pants that day at the hospital, he doubted the bike ride had been too strenuous for her. Which meant Just Julia wasn't comfortable with him seeing a perceived weakness. And he couldn't blame her. Not that he knew her all that well, but he was on a first-name basis with inadequacy and recognized the feeling when he saw it.

"Have you dated much?" he asked.

"I dated a man in med school."

Just one? That long ago? "So what happened?"

"He was my professor. I was a little out of my element and he knew it. I'd never been in a relationship before, and he convinced me that what we had was special."

"And it wasn't?"

"Apparently not. After a couple of months, I found out that he not only was married but also had a history of sleeping with his students, and I was just one more in the books for him. I felt like such a fool when I finally figured it out. I vowed never to be in a relationship again without knowing every single detail about the man I was with."

"So you're just bad at picking the right guys." He reached out and lifted her chin from where it had sunk. What he really wanted to do was pay an office visit to this professor and bust a textbook over his scholarly, philandering head. "That doesn't mean you're a fool."

"Really? Because the way I was raised, lack of knowledge is the same thing as foolishness. I let my emotions rule my head and wound up completely in the dark about the type of man he was."

"Trust me. You won't be a fool again. I already told you I'd help."

"Actually, I think I'm doing pretty well on this bike, which means you don't get to pick my date after all."

"What about your Aunt Freckles? Is she still pulling out all the stops to get your dating life up and running?"

"Don't even get me started on that. Last Wednesday, I met one of my online matches at the hospital cafeteria during my lunch break, and—"

"Hold up. You had some guy you don't even know meet you where you work?" Kane was stunned. He knew she was inexperienced, but this was just careless. He didn't remember jumping off the bike, but he was pacing back and forth along the shoulder of the road before he realized she was clearly not as bothered by the situation as he was.

"Did I break some secret dating rule?" She crossed her arms over her chest, and he tried not to stare at the way the gesture forced her thighs to balance the bike between them.

"Of course you did. The rule is Stranger Danger 101." His legs grew tense and his stomach dropped at the potential risk she'd put herself in. "Why didn't you just give him directions to your house and provide him with duct tape and the blueprints to your basement so he could hide your body?"

She tightened her blond ponytail. "Don't you think you're overreacting a bit?"

"Better this reaction than the one I'd have if I found you buried underneath your back porch inside a fifty-five-gallon drum."

"Maybe you shouldn't watch so many serial killer documentaries."

"And maybe you shouldn't set yourself up to become a victim." Okay, even he knew his outburst was over the top. But sometimes his imagination got the best of him, and more than sometimes he spoke without thinking. Plus, seeing her straddling the red lateral tube was doing something funny to his blood flow. And his jeans.

"Kane, I was in a public place. With plenty of people around. And Aunt Freckles taught me how to do background checks after that coffee fiasco with the open relationships man. The guy from Wednesday was harmless. In fact, he was a seventh-grade science teacher."

"Then what was wrong with him?" Kane asked, stopping himself from firing off more inappropriate questions. *Was he ugly? Had he lied about his height? Did he chew with his mouth open? Did he completely lose his cool and overreact at the thought of her going out with another man?*

"How do you know something was wrong with him?"

Kane tilted his head forward and raised an eyebrow.

Julia let out a breath. "Okay, so he was a little too full of himself. But in his defense, I didn't quite meet his expectations."

Now *that* was hard to believe. If you asked Kane, Julia probably exceeded most guys' expectations. She was definitely out of Kane's league, for sure. Of course, given his track record, it seemed like only gold diggers and wannabe starlets were the types of women in his lineup. Good thing he'd retired from relationships when he'd retired from professional baseball.

"How could you possibly not be what he was looking for?" He pulled off his wool sweater and handed it to her when he saw her shiver. Then he thought of a better way to warm her up and mentally kicked himself. "Actually, let's get this thing turned around and you can tell me on the ride back. It's getting pretty cold."

He climbed back on, and as they pedaled more fluidly, Julia kept him entertained with the story of her lunch date who had talked nonstop throughout their meal and had regaled her with tales about the importance of science and how he thought it was very commendable that she was studying to get her nursing degree and how he'd almost gone into premed but he thought he could do more good molding young minds.

"Wait. Why did he think you were getting a nursing degree?"

"Apparently, when I'd used the dating app to change my profile questionnaire, I checked some wrong buttons. My smartphone is really frustrating. It's always deleting texts and mismarking my entries and doing that autocorrect thing. I'll never figure the damn thing out."

He doubted it was an issue with her phone so much as her fingers. "So, did you correct him and tell him you were a neurosurgeon?"

"I did."

"And?"

"And he laughed and didn't believe me at first. Then he spouted off some statistics for med school and how hard it was to get accepted to a good program. He went on to inform me that he'd been rejected by several of them, so he was pretty sure they didn't just let any pretty face in. I was wearing my surgical scrubs, so I had to pull out my hospital ID badge to prove it."

Good. Served the pompous knucklehead right. The only thing that didn't make Kane want to throw a fastball at the guy's stomach was his agreement with the assessment of Julia's pretty face. "How'd he take it when you put him in his place?"

"Let's just say some men are intimidated by my education and my job. At least, that's what I have to assume, since he hasn't contacted me since then. Well, not including the email he sent me right after lunch saying I should have been more honest and he didn't think we had enough in common."

"Sounds like it was his loss." Kane sure hoped Julia didn't think she'd done anything wrong. Other than apparently giving Freckles her passcode so her aunt could download that ridiculous app, knowing full well Julia's limited abilities with electronics. Of course, he'd had to fix her phone several times and now knew her passcode, as well.

"Maybe. The good news is that I only have one more date to go before Aunt Freckles will let me call it a day with this whole experiment of hers."

"Is that what it is? An experiment?"

He couldn't see Julia, but imagined her shrugging. "Experiment, charade, demonstration of why I'm better off being alone. I prefer to refer to it as anything that doesn't imply my failure."

"Oh, we're back to that word again?"

"We are. Which means it's your turn now to tell me about your shortcomings."

He turned in to the driveway, and he was half hoping the twins were outside to beg for a ride or a wrestling match or even a tutorial session on advanced mathematics—

anything to distract Julia from finding out what a disaster he'd made of his life.

"Too bad I can't go into more detail about that right this second," he said. "Now that I've lost this bet, I've got a pie-eating contest on the line as my last shot at redemption." He parked the bike and held it steady while she climbed off.

"I hope that someday you will tell me," she said, not making any move to walk away from him. "Or if not me, maybe a professional therapist."

"I don't need a shrink to tell me what's wrong with me. I already know. I've made my choices, and I'm moving on and trying to be happy with my new job. My new life."

He began walking toward the house and was shocked when her delicate hand grabbed under his biceps to pull him back. Her lips pursed in seriousness. "Kane, I meant what I said in there at dinner. I really think you are incredibly talented. What you've done to my house is just amazing. I hope you can put to rest all those ghosts that are haunting you and take some pride in your work."

It was more than ghosts haunting him. Growing up, he knew that, in his family, he wasn't the smartest—like his brother Kaleb—or the best-behaved—like his brother Kev—or even the toughest—like his sister Kylie. He definitely wasn't the friendliest—like his brother Bobby Junior. Sports were the only thing Kane'd been good at—the area where he excelled. The feeling of his long-standing inadequacy in all other aspects of his life had been relieved only on the pitching mound. When he'd lost that, he'd lost himself.

Julia's bad luck with relationships was nothing compared to Kane's career setback. How could he explain that as much as he wanted to be successful like the rest of his siblings, he didn't have the brain power or the patience to do so? He could never make someone like Dr. Smarty-Pants, who learned to remove brain tumors with robotic arms because challenges were fun for her, understand what it was like for someone who'd barely graduated high school.

He couldn't.

But he could still appreciate her going to bat for him and trying to make him feel like he wasn't some old has-been. "You know, I meant to thank you for what you said at dinner. Nobody's ever defended me like that before. I appreciate it."

"I don't think anyone else appreciated it. They were all so quiet after I spoke up. I hope I didn't offend them."

He laughed. "They were quiet because they've never heard anyone defend me like that, either. At least, not anyone who isn't related to me."

"Well, it *does* make me feel better to know that your family is willing to stick up for you."

Just then the front door opened, and Aiden launched himself off the porch. "You won the bet, right, Dr. Julia?"

"I sure did. My bike-riding instructor was a little bossy, but after a while, I got the hang of it," she said, winking at Kane over the nine-year-old's head.

"Our new bike was fun, right, Uncle Kane?" Caden jumped down three steps in a single leap.

"Once she finally learned to relax and trust me, it was fun," Kane replied, winking back.

It was true. Riding the bike with her had been exciting, to say the least. He thought about his sister Kylie's accusation in the café the other day. His family was right. Kane hadn't been fun for a long time.

But today he was actually enjoying himself. At least,

he had been, before he saw the headlights of Renault's Jeep pulling into the driveway.

"Are you sure you don't wanna go door-bustin' with me?" Aunt Freckles asked when she dropped Julia off in front of her house later that night.

"Positive. I'd rather go against Bobby Chatterson and Aiden Gregson in a pie-eating challenge than fight off a line of people in a crowded department store."

Freckles chuckled. "Kane was certainly giving them a run for their money. That is, until he decided to shove his pumpkin pie into Lieutenant Renault's face."

"Oh, Freckles, I doubt he *decided* to do anything of the sort. Kane said it was an accident, and he looked pretty upset with himself afterward."

"It wasn't himself he was upset with, Sug." Her aunt checked her lipstick in the rearview mirror. "Kane was getting pretty territorial from the moment that Renault fellow walked in the door."

"I think he just feels a bit protective around his nieces. He was hovering over me when I was holding little Gracie, too. When he squished his way onto the sofa and sat down right between me and Lieutenant Renault, I had to remind him that I've taken classes on pediatrics and knew how to hold a baby."

Julia couldn't be positive because the only light in the car was from the overhead dome, but she was pretty sure one of Freckles's painted-on eyebrows was much higher than the other.

A howl rumbled from inside her house, and Julia saw Mr. Donut's black nose pressed up against the fogged-up glass of her living room window. For a dog with such stubby legs, he sure had an impressive ability to jump onto the white plastic patio chair she was temporarily using in place of an actual sofa.

"When are you going to tell Kane to take his dog home?" Freckles asked.

"I keep meaning to. But every time the subject comes up, there's always some sort of distraction, and we get to talking about something else." She didn't want to say out loud that the distraction was usually the way he looked in his sexy flannel shirts. At least on her end. She was beginning to suspect Kane had some issues with his attention span. The poor man changed the subject every time she brought up therapy. He surely wouldn't appreciate her diagnosing him with ADHD, even if she was a neurologist.

"If you ask me, Sug, I think you like having that grumpy ol' guy around a lot more than you let on."

"Kane's not that grumpy... Oh. You meant the dog." She hoped her aunt couldn't see the flush of heat blossoming on her cheeks. "Yes, I do rather like having Mr. Donut for company. You know my father was terribly allergic to animals, so I'm finally getting to fulfill a childhood dream with only half the responsibility. Maybe I'll wind up getting one of my own if my schedule ever allows it."

Freckles tsk-tsked. "That blasted schedule of yours. If I've said it once, I've said it a bajillion times. You need to make time for the important stuff, Sug."

"Important stuff like what?"

"Like making your house a home."

"You're right, as usual. In fact, Kane brought over a few decorating catalogs for me, and I've been meaning to visit that furniture store in Boise."

"Ugh. That's not what I meant, child."

Julia knew she was supposed to pick up on some hidden

meaning here, but she preferred things in black and white. Why couldn't everyone just speak more literally?

"How's the An Apple a Day dating service going?" her aunt asked.

"Not bad." She shrugged, thinking Freckles had the same tendency as Kane to switch conversation topics before Julia could figure out what message they were trying to convey.

"*Not bad* isn't the same thing as *good*."

"That's why I said *not bad*. But do I really have to take a date to that hospital gala?"

"Unless you want people to talk, you should go with someone. Now that Kane lost that bet to you, I wonder if he is taking anyone."

"I wouldn't know. He made it pretty clear that he has no interest in dating or socializing in general. Then after I proved that I could ride a bike, I didn't want to be a poor sport and bring the subject up."

"Well, let's try to find out, shall we?"

"Why?"

"Because…oh, never mind. You let Aunt Freckles worry about it. But right now, those sales aren't going to shop themselves. I've got to get going to make it to the Midnight Madness Blowout."

Julia gave her aunt a hug and exited the car. Maybe she could approach the subject with Kane by appeasing his ego and telling him he could still pick whom she took as her plus-one. Lord knew she wasn't finding anyone suitable on her own and now that Freckles brought up the idea of him bringing another woman to the gala, the last thing Julia wanted was to have to sit at some table all by herself, watching as he bestowed that sexy little smirk of his on someone else. Forewarned was forearmed, right?

Forcing the conversation could have other advantages, as well. Like reminding her that Kane wasn't in the running himself, no matter how much she loved being welcomed by his family or how good his rear end had looked on that bike seat in front of her.

Chapter Ten

"What do you mean, Freckles thinks you should go out dancing?" Kane shook his head at Julia. "Do you *know* how to dance?"

"I took classical ballet when I was younger." She squared her shoulders, ready to shoot down his arguments and his negative attitude. It had been only a week since she'd proven herself more than capable of riding a tandem bicycle. He of all people should know she wasn't one to give up. "And I've been watching a few videos on YouTube. I think I'll be able to manage."

Julia passed Kane an opened cardboard container, and he grimaced at its contents. "So, who's the lucky guy who gets to take you dancing?"

When she'd pulled up at seven that evening, Julia had been surprised to see Kane's Bronco at the curb in front of her house, all the downstairs lights blazing. She'd brought home takeout from the tiny Chinese restaurant near the hospital and had just offered to share some of her dinner with him when the conversation segued from the baseboards he'd finished sanding into her plans for the weekend.

"I don't know yet. That whole online thing hasn't been going according to plan. My last match was a sixty-eight-year-old pharmaceutical sales rep from Rexburg who lives with his mother. PharmBandit889 said his mom wouldn't approve of him dating a modern woman who worked outside the home and asked if I'd be willing to quit."

"What'd you tell him?" He sniffed the sweet-and-sour sauce before dipping his spring roll in it.

"I told him there's no way I'd quit my job for any man. Or his mother. Anyway, Freckles said if I get dressed up and go to a club, I'll find plenty of men to dance with."

"By yourself? No way." This overprotective big brother role Kane had taken on was grating on every one of Julia's only-child nerves. How else was she supposed to find a date and get over this stupid attraction to him? She was willing to try anything at this point.

"Not alone," she defended herself. "Your sister Kylie called me the other day and said Luke's friend Lieutenant Renault asked for my phone number. I was thinking he might want to go with me."

The chopstick in Kane's hand snapped in half. "You do *not* want to go to a bar with Renault."

"Why not? His rank really isn't that much below mine. He's an officer. I don't think the Navy will have a problem with fraternization. Besides, it's not a bar. It's a dance club."

"A dance club with a bar inside. Those places are meat markets. And going with some hotshot like Renault? It'd be like sending a lamb into a den of lions with their alpha leader as her date. What are Kylie and Freckles thinking, making a suggestion like that?"

Kane tossed a piece of General Tso's tofu to Mr. Donut, who caught it easily before changing his mind and letting the small cube roll off his tongue and onto the floor.

"You know, I really don't think you should feed him from the table like that," Julia said.

"This isn't exactly a table." Kane used his hands to jiggle the floppy plywood balanced on top of two sawhorses.

"Good point. That reminds me. Aunt Freckles invited her friend Cessy Walker to go furniture shopping with us in Boise tomorrow. Maybe I'll look for something more permanent for the dining room."

"First your aunt wants you to go to a bar with some overly muscled, overly confident, macho SEAL," he said before shoving a scoop of vegetable fried rice in his mouth. She didn't point out the similarity between Renault's build and his, although Kane definitely had the advantage when it came to making her legs wobbly. The man seemed determined to find fault with Luke's friend, so maybe he knew something Julia didn't. "And now she wants to subject you to the self-appointed Sugar Falls socialite and decorating queen?"

"What's wrong with Cessy Walker? Aunt Freckles says she can be a bit on the snobbish side, but that she has impeccable taste and good style."

"Nothing's wrong with her, exactly. She's nice enough, I guess, and she means well. But when she and your aunt get together, their opinions become a force of nature, and you can be assured they'll steamroller right over you. A whole team of Navy SEALs like your dance partner Renault wouldn't be able to stop them."

"He's not *my* Renault. And why are you in such a bad

mood all of a sudden? Surely you aren't intimidated by Cessy Walker?"

Kane rolled his eyes. "Oh please. I could handle that queen bee with one arm tied behind my back."

"Great. Then maybe you can go with us tomorrow?" Julia issued the challenge and then held her breath. The steamroller picture he'd just painted didn't seem all that appealing, and she wouldn't mind having him there for backup.

"No way. I handle Cessy Walker best by avoiding her."

"You can't tell me you're afraid of a little sixty-something-year-old lady."

"Don't let *her* hear you refer to her as being in her sixties. And I'm not afraid of the woman. At least, not when it's just her. But last spring, she and your charming aunt got together and planned a bachelor auction to raise funds for the new firehouse the city's building just north of downtown."

"So? What's wrong with that?" To Julia, charities and fund-raisers were an integral part of giving back to the community, and it seemed normal that one of the wealthier socialites in town would lead the noble charge.

"What's *wrong* is that they didn't tell any of the so-called bachelors what they were doing and then tricked us all into getting up on stage when the auction started."

"Us?" Julia's lips twitched completely of their own accord. She'd bet the antisocial Kane Chatterson didn't like being thrown into the limelight one bit. But instead of feeling sorry for him, a small part of her wished she could've been a fly on the wall to see him forced out of his comfort zone like that. And to see how high the bidding got. "You mean, you were one of the bachelors?"

"Not for long, I wasn't," he said, wiping his mouth with a paper napkin. "I walked out the door before the opening bids even started. I got an earful about it the next day from my sister, along with half the women in town. They said I was being a spoilsport and uncharitable. I said I was being myself, and they got what they should've expected."

"What would it have hurt to go along with it?"

"What would it have hurt?" Kane took off his ball cap and ran his fingers through his short-cropped hair. "What if someone had actually bid on me?"

"Then you would have taken her on the date she paid for. You know—" she pointed her empty soda bottle at him, trying not to appear too giddy at the opening she'd been waiting for "—we talk about my dating life, but we never talk about yours."

He picked up their plates and carried them to the sink. "That's because there's nothing to talk about. Just like you, I'm not out looking for someone to share my life with. I'm much more comfortable being alone. Women, no offense, have a tendency to complicate things and push for more than I'm willing to give."

Wow. It was no more black-and-white than that. He was making it more than clear that he didn't return her feelings—whatever those were. Even she didn't know if this was just physical attraction or something more.

And did she sound that defensive when she'd made a similar argument? A kernel of pity wedged itself in her chest, and she wondered if he'd also been burned by a bad relationship. But at the same time, she envied him for knowing exactly what he didn't want and for not letting anyone tell him he had to be with a woman to be happy. Even if Julia lost out because of it.

"No offense taken," she said, putting her professional face back in place. "So I guess that means you won't be bringing a date to the Sugar and Shadow Shindig?"

"You guess right. I'm not about to let one of my family members talk me into online dating or going out to bars to meet people."

"Again, it's a dance club, not a bar. And it's because I promised my aunt that I'd give finding a date a solid effort. I'm not like you, Kane. I don't like to let people down or give something less than one hundred percent."

He was standing in front of the sink, making it difficult to see his expression. But there was no missing the sudden tensing of his shoulders. Without turning toward her, he asked, "Are you saying I don't give things one hundred percent?"

Uh-oh. Now she'd gone and insulted him. Maybe she should've taken a page out of his book and not even attempted to be friendly to him. Clearly she wasn't getting any better at making friends, no matter how much of an endeavor she made. She stood and crossed the room. "I didn't mean it like that. I just meant that you seem comfortable with the status quo. That's not a bad thing, Kane. I actually envy that about you. Here, let me help you with the dishes."

She put her hand on his arm, and instead of jerking it away, which would have been something she'd expect if he were angry with her, he kept it eerily still.

"They're already done," he said, his voice as tight as his motionless biceps. There went that weird tingling in her head, followed by the sensation making its way down her neck. She quickly pulled her hand from the warm flannel of his sleeve and mentally grasped at some sort of neutral topic to shift the conversation into something that would make sense to her, that wouldn't send her body into sensory overload.

"I've been noticing that you've done quite a few dishes around here since I've moved in."

"How do you know that I'm the one doing them?" He twisted a dish towel in his hands, but kept his body and attention planted firmly in place in front of her kitchen sink.

"Because I didn't think the plumber or any of the roofers you hired would clean up my messes after I leave."

"Sorry about that." He began to wipe down the perfectly spotless counters. "It's just that I don't like being surrounded by a lot of clutter or chaos when I'm working. It can be very distracting for me."

"Has anyone ever suggested that you might have some issues with your attention span?"

"Only every teacher since kindergarten."

"Have you been formally diagnosed with ADHD?"

He looked up to her ceiling, and the corners of his taut mouth dropped ever so slightly. "Yeah. When I was seven years old and still not reading, my parents took me to the doctor. They prescribed some medicine, and it helped me focus a little better in school, but it made me sick to my stomach, and I had problems falling asleep."

"But there are so many doses and different types of medications that it takes a while to get it all dialed in correctly."

"If you say so." He went back to the counter, using the dish towel to scrub at an invisible mark. "Will you hand me that bottle of cleaner from under the sink?"

This time, though, she wouldn't let his penchant for changing topics sidetrack her. "Did you ever try anything else to help with your ADHD?"

When he saw she wasn't going to indulge him in his counter-cleaning smoke-and-mirrors routine, he let out a breath, turning to lean against the cabinet. "Mom and Dad tried it all. Behavioral coaches, tutors, breathing exercises, positive reinforcement. I could deal with it okay enough at home and when I played sports, but anything that required me to be still and concentrate was too difficult."

"That's very unfortunate," she said in her best medical professional voice. She doubted a man like Kane would appreciate her pity. "Have you done anything about it since you've reached adulthood? There are new medicines and resources now that could be quite beneficial."

"I deal with it by staying busy and keeping other people's houses clean so I can get my work done."

Julia didn't want to push him, not when he was so close to revealing such an integral part of himself that surely had shaped his life and the way he saw the world. But she'd get her answers eventually. She always did. In the meantime, she would allow him to change the subject back to her.

"I should be better about that," she said, only somewhat remorseful. "I grew up with housekeepers and parents who wanted the house pristine enough to grace the pages of *Architectural Digest*. I never even lived in a dorm on campus. I moved straight from their house to the officers' quarters, where we would have random inspections. This is my first time living on my own, and I guess I went a little over-the-top with my rebellion against tidiness. Are you going to add housekeeping services to your invoice?"

"I should." He smirked, and Julia was relieved that the earlier tension was losing steam. Mr. Donut let out a yawn from underneath the pseudotable, drawing their attention.

"Just as long as you issue me a credit for all the pet-sitting I've been doing for you these past few weeks." She tried to form her lips into a matching smirk.

Kane shook his head. "What pet-sitting?"

"Your dog. The one you leave here every night?"

"Jules, I don't have a dog. And if I did, I certainly wouldn't bring him to work with me."

"Hello?" She pointed to the hound with the droopy ears. "What about Mr. Donut?"

"What about him?" Kane crossed his arms over his chest. "He's not *my* dog."

"Then whose is he?"

"I thought he was *yours*."

"I've never owned a pet in my life."

The animal in question let out a whiff of air, and Kane waved his hand in front of his nose. "It looks like you own one now."

"No. I only let him stay here because I thought he belonged to you and I was doing you a favor."

"What kind of person would leave their pet at someone else's house without asking?"

"I don't know. I thought it was odd myself, but you're kind of a mystery."

Kane lowered his chin. "I'm a mystery?"

"Not in a bad way. I meant you're interesting. You're not what I'm used to."

"What are you used to?"

"Obviously I'm not used to any of this." She waved her hand around the house. "Living on my own, finding a date for the hospital fund-raiser, dealing with my well-meaning aunt, who keeps buying me tacky makeup by the way, and her socialite friend." *Lusting after my sexy contractor.*

"Just tell them you're not bringing a plus-one."

"But Aunt Freckles will be disappointed."

"She'll get over it. You need to start standing up for yourself, Jules."

"Maybe."

"Not maybe. Yes. So that problem's solved. What else aren't you used to?"

"I'm not used to taking care of someone else's dog..."

"Mr. Donut isn't *mine*."

"Well, you named him," he chuckled. "And he certainly follows you around like he's yours."

"That's only because I feed him human food. He sleeps in *your* bed."

"You mean the bed with the comforter on it that you bought me?"

She'd meant to say the words jokingly, but suddenly the teasing glint in Kane's eye was gone. It'd been replaced with something she couldn't quite name, but whatever it was had his pupils dilated and made his voice grow quiet when he said, "Speaking of your bed, I don't think it's a good idea for me to be working here so late anymore."

Her heart dropped. "Why not?"

"Because every time you're around, I can't focus on what I'm working on."

He took a step closer, and she had to angle her chin to look up at him. "Do you think that has something to do with your ADHD?"

"No. I think it has something to do with your bow-shaped lip," he said before closing the distance between them.

His kiss took her by surprise. She gasped and he pushed against her open mouth with his tongue as she let him inside, allowing herself to grow accustomed to the feel of him before tentatively kissing him back.

When she responded, he groaned and slid his hands inside her cashmere cardigan, planting his palms on either side of her waist. Her breasts pressed against him and the rest of her followed suit, molding itself along each contour of his body.

She'd once had to administer a dose of epinephrine when one of her patients had suffered an allergic reaction. She imagined the shock of having the adrenaline hit one's bloodstream felt exactly like this. A burst of pure energy raced through her veins, and she had to have more. Gripping his shoulders to steady herself, Julia tilted her head to get a better angle, a better taste.

Kane must have maneuvered her against the kitchen counter, because she felt the cool granite against the back of her waist, where her shirt and sweater had lifted. He groaned again, and she heard a soft thud of something hitting the floor. But it was too difficult to think about the sounds around her when her heart was pounding so thoroughly in her ears.

Julia felt something brush against her shin, and Kane stumbled back. She looked down to see Mr. Donut wedging his thick body between them and using his nose to root around inside a to-go container that had fallen off the counter. The dog successfully slurped up the lo mein noodles, seemingly having no concern for what he'd just interrupted.

She exhaled, then immediately closed her lips to keep Kane from seeing how desperately she wanted him to return to them. But there was no need to concern herself with Kane even glancing in her direction. His eyes briefly passed over the dog before lifting to the ceiling and finally landing on the emptiness outside her kitchen window. "I, uh, better go," he said to the darkened glass behind her.

It took a second to find her voice. When she finally did, she was barely able to rasp out the word, "Okay."

He turned and walked toward the front door, giving

no excuse and making no apology. And surprisingly, she didn't want to hear either. For a woman who prided herself on finding a logical reason for everything, Julia didn't think she could bear hearing his contrite explanation or facing the realization that when it came to men, she'd once again failed to see the signs and had made another mistake.

Kane would voluntarily have undergone surgery on his good shoulder if it would've meant tuning out Cessy and Freckles talking about the Sugar and Shadow Shindig at the nearby table inside the Cowgirl Up Café. Especially because he knew it was just a matter of time before they brought up Julia and who she'd be bringing to the dinner dance as her date.

Jealousy spread over his skin just as easily as Freckles's homemade huckleberry jam over the hot biscuit on his plate. And hearing the chorus for Rudolph the Red-Nosed Reindeer chirping out of the overhead speakers was making him feel anything but jolly.

Kane knew last night's kiss was a bad idea five seconds before he'd moved in for it. But as usual, his actions beat his brain to the punch. Then, instead of apologizing like a rational person would have done, he'd flown out of her house like a runner stealing second base when the catcher already had the ball. He drove home the same way he'd lived out his twenties—with reckless abandon. Nothing had been able to slow his racing pulse, his racing mind. Then, refusing to imagine how much more would've happened if the dog hadn't interrupted them, he'd gone straight to his garage and stayed up most of the night busting his knuckles installing a high-performance camshaft and valve train on the Bronco. He forced himself to do mental calculations of cubic inch displacement and to read long-winded owner's manuals rather than think of how perfectly Julia's compact body had felt against his. Or how hot her tongue had been when she'd met his demanding rhythm.

And now, twelve hours later, he couldn't forget a single sensation, a single spark.

Dr. Smarty-Pants had been warm and passionate in his arms, her hands curious, her mouth exploring his. Those lips of hers feeling as if they'd been made for kissing him...

Sleigh bells tinkled behind him, and he turned toward the doors, which were actually covered with wrapping paper and decorated with bows to resemble Christmas presents. Marcus Weston stepped inside, and most of the customers in the Cowgirl Up Café turned to look at the former point guard for the men's basketball team at a Division I college. The one scouts expected to be a first-round pro-draft pick, until he enlisted in the Marine Corps halfway through his senior year. Marcus still walked with a limp, not quite used to his new prosthetic foot.

"'Sup, Legend," the man said when he reached Kane's table.

Kane stood up to shake Marcus's hand. "Don't call me that. Not here."

"Because none of these local town folks know who you are?" Only the lower half of Marcus's body had been engulfed in flames after his fighter jet had crash-landed and exploded in a training exercise over a year ago—which meant the man's black eyebrows could still be easily raised with sarcasm. "Anyway, where's this wilderness guide we're supposed to meet?"

"Alex should be here soon." Kane took a gulp of his decaf coffee, wishing he hadn't arranged to meet some of the guys from the PTSD group at Julia's aunt's restaurant before the mountain biking trip. But then, how was he supposed to know he'd go and ruin everything by pushing their relationship way past the friendship zone?

The bitter aftertaste of the brew burned its way down his throat, and he slid the complimentary basket of buttermilk biscuits away from him, deciding he wasn't in the mood to eat, after all. He couldn't even enjoy his breakfast anymore, knowing that the café owner talking to her friend a few tables down was only one phone call away from finding out that he'd put the moves on her niece last night.

"You're going riding with us, right?" Marcus took a seat opposite him in the booth and opened the laminated menu.

"Actually, I'm not operating on much sleep today and might skip out after Alex gets everyone set up on bikes." God, not only was his morning meal ruined, but also he couldn't even think of bicycles without thinking of Julia now.

"C'mon, man. Dr. Gregson says one of the best things for our recovery is to get outside in nature."

"And he's probably right." However, Kane didn't have PTSD, and no amount of nature would cure him from thinking about how Julia's narrow, firm body fit so well against his. In fact, he'd probably think about it so much, he'd end up riding his bike off a big rock. "But it's not like you actually need me today."

"I'm from Miami, Legend. We don't do mountains in Florida. In fact, most of the guys coming on the trip today are from the big cities and think they'll end up suffocating in this fresh air. The only reason they agreed to come is that they like hanging out with you." Marcus pointed a long brown finger at him. "Don't blow them off, man."

Kane cleared his throat, trying to dislodge the knot of

guilt that had wedged itself inside him. "You said *they* like hanging out with me."

"Personally, I think you can be a real downer, and it probably wouldn't hurt for you to get laid." Marcus smiled, and Kane pulled a muscle in his neck trying to look over to see if Freckles or any of the other customers had heard what the man just said. "I only stay in the group so I can tell people that I bench-press more than Legend Chatterson."

"That's because I have a bad shoulder," Kane grumbled.

"At least you still have a shoulder." Marcus reached into the basket and pulled out a biscuit. "I'm missing a foot and still outran you last week on the track."

This was why his brother-in-law Drew had convinced Kane to come to his therapy group. He knew his patients needed motivation to regain their physical fitness. But Drew also knew that Kane needed to rise to a challenge once in a while.

"You're not going to beat me today," Kane shot back, recognizing the competitive glint in Marcus's determined eyes.

Just as Monica stopped by to take their order, the bells tinkled over the door again, and Kane gulped when he saw Julia walk into the café. Actually, she blasted in, still wearing her headphones, which obviously weren't completely plugged in, judging by the way the saxophone riffs spewed out of the tiny speaker on the iPod strapped to her arm. Kane had to give her credit for her improved taste in music, but a sudden jolt of energy crackled through his already restless muscles, and he had to force himself not to run out the door. Or worse, run straight toward her and kiss her all over again.

"Sug," Freckles hollered over the sound, making even

Scooter Deets, who was hard of hearing, take notice of Julia's arrival. "Turn that dang thing off and come meet Cessy Walker."

He saw her take a step back, her eyes darting around at the audience now looking her way. Kane shot to his feet and made it to her side in under five steps. His hand reached for her arm to hold the iPod steady as he shoved the earplug cord home. Julia's arm didn't jerk back at his touch—which was a relief—but her green eyes rounded as the music screamed its way into her ears.

She pulled the headphones off and made several attempts to swipe at the device's screen before finally getting the thing powered down.

"Thanks," she said. He wasn't sure if the flush on her cheeks was from embarrassment at everyone watching them or if it was leftover from how he'd behaved last night.

Or maybe it was because she'd obviously been out running, as her workout clothes and sneakers suggested.

"No problem." He tried to smile, but it felt too forced. Too awkward. Like everyone in this restaurant would know what they'd done last night.

Well, what *he'd* done.

Before he could stop them, his eyes moved of their own accord to her lips, and he remembered exactly how active a participant Just Julia had been last night. He corrected himself again. What he'd started, but what *they'd* done. Both of them. Together.

"Sug." Freckles stood, a perfectly coiffed Cessy Walker trailing behind her, and walked toward them. Kane took a couple steps back, retreating to his table while he still had the chance. Unfortunately, it wasn't until after he sat down in the safe confines of his booth that he realized he was now trapped only a few feet away from them as Freckles stood there with her socialite best friend, making introductions and talking about formal wear and hairstyles and beauty shop appointments.

Some of the confidence had even drizzled out of Marcus's smirk when it didn't appear that the three women would be moving anytime soon, thereby allowing the new waitress to take their breakfast order.

With nothing to do but wait this out, Kane settled back in his seat and allowed his eyes to roam over Julia's body. She was wearing black spandex pants that hugged every inch of her toned legs. Her long-sleeved white T-shirt with NAVY stamped across her breasts wasn't quite long enough to cover her rear end, and Kane's right knee bounced in double-time thinking about how close his hands had been to those sweet curves last night.

"Julia, honey, we're putting you and your date at the head table," Cessy said, the word *date* hurled its way into Kane's inappropriate thoughts and snapped him back to the present.

"That's the thing I actually wanted to speak to you both about," Julia replied, but instead of looking at the two women, she was staring at Kane. Was she going to stand up to them? He nodded at her and gave his fist a small pump in solidarity. Julia took a breath and continued. "I've decided not to bring a date to the gala."

"I had a feeling it was going to come down to this." But instead of looking annoyed, Cessy's bright red lips were spread in a satisfied grin. Julia's eyes grew wide, her smile tentative as though she was surprised at how quickly she'd accomplished her goal.

But before Kane could lift his fist again in support of her victory, Cessy continued. "Your Aunt Freckles and I have been putting together a list of some single gentlemen that you can bring."

Kane braced his forearms on the table and Julia crossed her arms in front of her chest, her defensive stance actually drawing more attention to her chest. Or at least, Kane's attention. "Like who?"

"How about Carla Patrelli's brother?" Freckles asked. "He just moved here recently from Chicago."

"Isn't that the guy who got drunk at karaoke night at the VFW and asked every woman in the place to sing a Bee Gees duet with him?" Kane shook his head at Julia. "You're not going with him. He's obviously a player."

Freckles and Cessy whispered to each other before the waitress began reading off her notepad. "There's Jake Marconi's friend who has that nice animal shelter out off Highway 18?"

"Carmen arrested him last month for running a dog fighting ring," Kane responded. "Next."

"Jeffrey what's-his-name, that Navy corpsman who was one of Chief Cooper's groomsmen?"

"Ran into him at the hospital a few months ago and he got married to his longtime girlfriend."

"Alex Russell?" Cessy suggested a bit too smugly. Kane should have known it was only a matter of time before the women suggested one of Sugar Fall's most sought-after bachelors. "He's single and you certainly can't object to one of your own poker buddies."

"Julia's too pretty for Alex," Kane said way too quickly, causing Freckles to arch one of her unnatural-looking eyebrows. "I mean, Alex likes his women more... plain and not so feminine."

"Then how about Vic Russell, his dad?" Freckles asked, her dreamy expression matching Cessy's. "He looks like Hugh Jackman's older brother."

Kane scrunched his nose. "He's twice her age, Freckles."

"Then I guess that takes us out of the running," Scooter

said to Jonesy, reminding Kane that everyone in the café was listening to this absurd conversation. Julia's mouth opened and closed as if she were looking for the opportunity and the right words to tell them all to butt out of her life. Yet her eyes pleaded with him to make this fiasco go away and he wanted to say, *See! I told you this is what they do when they get together. Steam. Roller.*

She'd laughed him off last night, but she certainly wasn't laughing now. He needed to do something to stop this runaway train from going completely off the rails. But before he could, the man across the table spoke up.

"I'll go with the hot doc." Marcus's smile widened even more than it had when they'd gone to the batting cages in Boise a couple of weeks ago and Kane had to remind the man that he couldn't be expected to hit *all* twelve of the balls because he used to be a pitcher, not a designated hitter.

"Hot doc?" Kane whipped his head back to the former basketball player. "Who calls her that?"

"Everyone in the physical rehab wing at the hospital," Marcus said as Freckles and Cessy began nodding in earnest and whipped out their seating chart. Then Marcus leaned across the table and put his hand up to his mouth before whispering, "Have you ever seen her in workout clothes?"

A green, jealous haze closed in around Kane and before he could ask Julia her opinion or stop the words from shooting out of his mouth, he all but shouted, "That's it. I'm going to take her my damn self."

Chapter Eleven

For a few days, Kane tried everything he could imagine to reconcile his desire to avoid both public events and complications with his building excitement that he was going to be taking Julia on an actual date. Of course, after he'd shot off his mouth in the Cowgirl Up Café that morning, he'd stormed out of the restaurant before the "hot doc" or her overprotective aunt could object—with Marcus Weston's laughter still ringing in his ears. Then he'd waited for a phone call, a text, a note taped to her front door or tied to Mr. Donut's new collar telling him that there was no way in hell she would be willing to attend the hospital gala with him. But no such message ever came, and he found his spirits lift each day that he'd successfully avoided her potential rejection.

In fact, he avoided her altogether, too afraid of crushing this unfamiliar feeling of hopefulness picking up speed in his chest. He waited until she left for work before going to her house. Then he'd purposely do minor repairs around the house, not wanting to become too engulfed in a project that would cause him to lose track of time so he could leave well before he anticipated her return.

Then, the following Tuesday, Freckles had sent him a text asking if they wanted to ride in the rented limo with her and Cessy. He fired off a reply saying that he would be driving them himself.

On Wednesday, when Kylie had left him a voice mail asking if he needed her to take his tux to the dry cleaner, he casually texted back that she could do whatever she wanted, but was secretly pleased to come home the following day to see it freshly pressed and hanging on his closet door.

On Friday, he'd accidentally caught a glimpse of a brand-new garment bag spread out on Julia's bed, and he'd slammed the door closed, refusing to acknowledge the way his palms itched to unzip the thing and take a peek at what Julia would be wearing to the gala.

For six days, they hadn't talked about the pending date, and they especially hadn't talked about their kiss. Actually, they hadn't talked at all. Kane had thought it was better this way, but now that he was parked in front of her house on Saturday evening, he had to wonder if not addressing the situation had only allowed his expectations to grow out of control.

He sat in his late-model Ford F-250, his more practical and comfortable vehicle, and pulled the gold watch out of his tuxedo pocket, more to fiddle with the latch than to check the time. He was still ten minutes early and couldn't very well sit in his idling truck all evening. And if he was a normal red-blooded male, he would've also decided that it was his lucky night.

But this wasn't luck. It was torture, pure and simple. He grabbed his tuxedo jacket off the front seat and slipped it on as he got out of his truck and walked up the front path to her porch. He inhaled the woodsy pine scent of the fresh wreath she'd bought—and he'd hung on her door—as he tried to regulate his breathing. He used the antique brass knocker, making a mental note to repair the doorbell, then heard a bark just before the front door opened to reveal a woman silhouetted by the golden chandelier light inside.

His breath caught at the wavy layers of blond hair framing her face and he cursed himself for not taking a peek inside that garment bag and preparing himself for how sexy she'd look tonight. But he had a feeling nothing could have prepared him for how his body would react to seeing her in that dress.

It wasn't gray, nor was it silver. It was satiny and smooth and clung to her curves. The color reminded him of his Grandpa Chatterson's antique revolver—the one Kane had never been allowed to touch. Her body was nearly as dangerous and his compulsion to break the rules for a chance to hold her was twice as strong.

Snow was starting to fall, yet he felt like he was burning up.

"Kane?" she asked, and he almost looked down at himself to make sure it really was him.

"Didn't recognize me in a tuxedo?" He tried to joke, but his voice was too raspy. His senses were too overwhelmed. This was really happening.

"Actually, I didn't recognize you in that truck. You didn't have to borrow someone's car," she said. "We could've taken mine."

"I didn't borrow it. I own it."

"Oh," was all she said.

It wasn't until he'd bent down to pet Mr. Donut that

Kane realized Julia was shifting from one strappy sandal to the other. He supposed she could be uncomfortable in such high heels, but a small part of him hoped she was just as nervous about the evening ahead as he was. Not that he wanted her to be anxious, but he'd feel a lot more secure if they were on common ground.

"Are you ready?" He stood, trying to wipe some of the hound's fur off his jacket sleeves.

"As ready as I'll ever be." She grabbed a small silver clutch and a scrap of fabric before stepping out onto the porch.

"Do you have a jacket?" Kane looked at her bare shoulders, one shade darker than the snow landing on her front yard.

"I've got a wrap. Besides, after spending the last thirty minutes trying to style my hair and squeeze into this dress, I'm way too hot even to think about a coat right now." That made two of them. But his temperature had nothing to do with getting dressed. "Freckles has been dead set on this makeover since I moved here. She made me promise not to wear my hair in a ponytail tonight, and I should've had it done professionally, but I was called in for an emergency surgery this morning and didn't get home in time to do much with it."

"I like it down," Kane said, reaching out to stroke one of the silky, wavy strands that framed her face. She looked up into his eyes and his head instinctively tilted toward hers, before Mr. Donut used his increasing bulk to nose his way between them.

The interruption caused Julia to take a step back and say, "I, uh, guess we'd better get going."

"Right." Kane shot the dog a reprimanding look, making a silent vow to never bring the interfering pooch another baked good, then used his own set of keys to lock her front door. He'd been locking this same door nearly every day for weeks, but never had it been more intimate than now, when she was standing beside him in a dress made for sin.

She pointed out the twinkling holiday lights decorating the storefronts along Snowflake Boulevard, but it took fifteen minutes to drive to the trendy Snow Creek Lodge, and during that time, he had to remind himself a dozen times to keep his hands off Julia. When they pulled up to the valet, he almost reminded the parking attendant of the same thing. Instead, he just gave the young guy a look that he hoped said, *Hands off, buddy. She's mine.*

As Kane walked around the truck, a strong breeze kicked up, and he saw her shiver. "Maybe I should've brought more than a skimpy wrap after all."

"Here." He wrapped his arm around her waist and pulled her in closer to his side, telling himself she felt too good to not belong there. And if he maybe shot the valet an eat-your-heart-out smirk, then so be it. "It'll be warmer when we get inside."

They walked into the lobby, and despite the fact that a ten-foot stone fireplace with a blazing fire took up the center of the room, Kane kept his arm around Julia. Heads turned in their direction as they made their way to the ballroom, and Kane experienced a flashback to when he used to attend major functions like this on a regular basis. He didn't hate it back then as much as he did now, but he'd never really loved the attention. He'd gone along with it for the team.

"All we have to do is get through the next couple of hours," he mumbled, hoping this shindig had a well-stocked bar.

"Are you talking to me or to yourself?" Julia asked, sticking to his side like pine tar on a batting glove.

"Both."

The big band orchestra was in full swing when they walked into the ballroom. Freckles was the first to rush over and greet them, and through the fabric of Julia's dress, Kane felt some of the tension leave her body. But only some.

Half the people he knew from living in Sugar Falls for the past year. The other half, Julia said she recognized from the hospital. A waiter handed them glasses of champagne, but Kane slipped the guy a twenty-dollar bill and asked him to bring a beer instead.

"You doing okay?" he asked, leaning in close enough to be heard over the music.

"I think so." Her smile seemed a bit forced. "Just stay close by."

With pleasure, he thought. By the time they made it to their table, Kane was positive his hand had left a permanent imprint on Julia's waist.

"You know what your dining room needs?" Freckles asked her niece as the waiter removed Kane's salad plate. "A pool table."

Everyone at their table had been giving Julia unsolicited opinions about her home remodel and decor while Kane had sat back and enjoyed the music. Of course, it helped that his sister and brother-in-law, as well as Luke and Carmen, were seated with them, providing him with an island of friends in this sea of social sharks.

It also helped that he was already on his second beer. All they had to do was get through the rest of dinner.

Cessy Walker returned to their table with Police Chief Matthew Cooper and Dr. Garrett McCormick, who'd both delivered speeches on the great work Shadowview Hospital did for active military and veterans. Their wives,

Maxine Cooper and Mia McCormick, came back from the ladies' room at the exact moment Cessy asked what she'd missed.

"I am not getting a pool table," Julia said, making Kane proud she was finally doing a better job of sticking up for herself and cementing the battle lines. "Besides, where would I put that antique armoire?"

"But men love pool tables," Freckles continued. "You can get one of those antler chandeliers to hang over it and maybe put up some classy-but-discreet neon beer signs."

"Is there such a thing as a classy-but-discreet beer sign?" Cessy challenged her.

"Another beer would be a blessing right about now," Kane mumbled, then jerked in surprise when Julia nudged him with her elbow. He chuckled, laying his arm along the back of her chair. He probably needed to get some real food in him to absorb the pale ale. He wasn't intoxicated or anything, but his fingers found the alcohol to be a convenient excuse for toying with the ends of Julia's loose hair as she turned to talk to Kylie about linen closets.

Freckles gave his hand a pointed look and then continued her campaign. "Are you saying you wouldn't want a pool table, Kane?"

"Not in the dining room, no."

"Which room would you put it in?" Luke Gregson asked.

"What about the bedroom?" Julia asked, and Kane's fingers froze.

"I dated a guy with a pool table in his bedroom once," Freckles said, then shrugged. "You could probably make it work if you skip the antlers and go for some tasteful artwork. Something painted on velvet, perhaps, to coordinate with the felt top."

"Sorry, Aunt Freckles. Are you still talking about the pool table? I thought we'd moved on to the armoire." Julia played with the stem of her champagne flute.

He remembered those same hands two weeks ago and how they'd felt against his waist when she'd been in his arms. Stroking his back, urging him closer. He couldn't remember the last time he'd held a woman so intimately.

Of course, he'd held plenty of women before, most of them unclothed, even. But with Julia it had been different. It didn't take a clinical psychologist like Drew to explain that Kane was simply wanting something he couldn't have.

If Mr. Donut hadn't interrupted them, they would've ended up in her bedroom for sure.

And if she didn't stop being so damn sexy and Kane didn't stop reliving that first kiss, they might still end up there.

Julia had once thought the guy looked hot in flannel, but nobody looked better than Kane Chatterson in a tuxedo. So good, in fact, even Chief Wilcox had given her a high five in the ladies' room earlier after asking Julia where she'd been hiding him. For the first time in twenty-nine years, she finally felt as though she could actually fit in somewhere.

Well, somewhere besides Kane's arms. His embrace had been the perfect fit. It had been almost two weeks since that passionate kiss in her kitchen and she could still feel the muscles in his waist tightening as her hands explored his torso. As his tongue explored her mouth.

When she'd run into him that morning in the Cowgirl Up Café, she'd been waiting for him to revert back to his brooding, moody personality so she could admit her failure to Freckles, then go home to her empty half-finished home and privately berate herself for falling for the wrong man. Again.

But his moodiness hadn't been directed at her, and she found herself sputtering in disbelief as he shot down one suggested date after another before declaring to the entire restaurant that he was going to take her to the gala.

After that, she threw herself into work and, as she checked her unreliable phone for a message from him calling the whole thing off, she told herself that no news was good news. She'd been so grateful to hear his knock on her door tonight, Julia had almost reenacted that reckless kiss again right there on her front porch. She made a mental note to bring home a doggie bag for Mr. Donut to reward him for his timely interruption.

The waiter had just removed their dinner plates when Kane's cell phone vibrated. He looked at the screen before frowning and mumbling something about people never leaving him alone. When the band launched into the first dance of the night, most of the couples at their table headed out to the parquet floor.

Except for when he'd been cutting into his prime rib, he'd spent most of the evening with his hands somewhere on her body. First on her waist, then in her hair and now on her shoulders. It felt as though someone had connected Julia to a morphine drip the moment she'd walked into the Snow Creek Lodge and she was floating through the evening on a dreamlike cloud of bliss.

Kane leaned closer. "I probably should have told you that I don't dance," he said. "Was that one of the requirements on your man list?"

She cleared her throat, then reached for her glass of ice water, thinking it would be more effective for her to throw it on her blushing face than just drink it. Why did he have to bring up that ridiculous subject again?

"No, but looking good in a tux wasn't on the list, either, and you aced it with that one." She clapped her hand over her mouth, mortified she'd let the thought slip out.

"Is that a fact?" His grin was all too pleased, and she had to straighten up in her chair to keep from hiding under the table. "Are you going to tell me what else is on it?"

She shrugged, the gesture not coming off as casual as she'd intended. "It doesn't matter now. I no longer need to look for any more dates."

Instead of retaining their teasing glint, his eyes stared her down, and *her* knee was now the one bouncing conspicuously under the table. The intensity of his gaze cut through her insides like a scalpel, and Julia had the sensation that she was completely exposed and raw.

Luckily his cell phone rang again, distracting him enough that he didn't see her little shudder. "Do you want to take that call?" Julia asked when he looked at the display screen.

"Hell, no, I don't want to take it," Kane said tightly. "But if I don't, he'll just keep calling me."

Cessy looked over Kane's shoulder at the screen, and Julia's eyes widened at the woman's invasion of his privacy. Well, Julia's eyes also widened at the fact that she'd forgotten they weren't completely alone at the table. But then Cessy patted Kane's arm in sympathy and said, "You might want to go outside and call him back."

"Will you excuse me?" he asked, and at her nod, he stood and left the table.

Julia's upbringing demanded that she not be so impolite as to ask Cessy who had called, but her curiosity demanded that she find out why he was so upset over it.

"Do you think Kane will be long?" Julia asked, fishing for information.

"It depends on why Charlie's calling," Cessy responded. Who was Charlie? Another client?

"He'd better not be giving our boy any grief." Freckles chimed in as she pulled off her high heels and replaced them with pink no-skid socks. "That stubborn man hates it when someone tries to force his hand."

Cessy nodded and pulled a pair of ballet-style slippers out of her beaded clutch. "He's too soft-hearted for his own good and needs someone to take care of him."

"Kane?" Julia asked. "You think Kane is too soft-hearted?"

Both women looked up from switching out their footwear. "Of course, Sug. Who else would we be talking about?"

"He doesn't seem very soft to me. Or like he needs anyone to protect him." Julia quickly peeked toward the entrance to ensure he wasn't coming this way. "In fact, last week he told me about how he managed to bail out of your bachelor auction without any assistance at all."

"Nah, we knew he wouldn't be willing to participate, anyway." Freckles used her reflection in her dinner knife to check her lipstick. "Kane Chatterson isn't exactly dating material."

"He's not?" Could've fooled Julia with the solicitous way he'd been acting tonight. But she'd been easily fooled before, and she wanted to get more information from them without giving the ladies any insight into her own feelings. "I'm sure plenty of women would have loved to go out on a date with him."

"Of course they would. But that doesn't mean they'd get their money's worth if any of them made a bid." Cessy waved at a group of elderly gentlemen.

Her aunt slightly lifted her sock-covered feet and gave them a wiggle. Oh goodness. These two ladies seemed as if they were ready to storm the dance floor. But Julia was determined to get answers before someone asked her sources of information for the next fox-trot. "So why trick Kane into participating?"

"We didn't trick him into *participating.*" Freckles sighed as if she was explaining Men 101. "We tricked him into blasting off that stage with enough white-hot anger to send a rocket ship into space."

Julia didn't point out the inaccuracies in her aunt's theory about emotions propelling interplanetary probes. She was too busy attempting to connect the cause and effect of these ladies' thought processes. "I'm afraid I don't see the logic in getting him mad for no reason."

"Here's how it works." Cessy placed a heavily jeweled hand on the linen tablecloth as if she were a battle commander outlining an attack route on a map. "Kane's the impulsive type that jumps to conclusions first, then asks questions later. He's also the type that feels especially guilty when he lets people down. Since guilt equals generous donation, we all got what we wanted."

"So, you're saying you staged the whole thing to get a small donation from him? Why didn't you just ask him for one?"

"Where's the fun in that?" Cessy's red-painted unnaturally plump lips were turned up in the same smug grin as when Kane had impulsively told them all he was going to be her date for the gala. The hairs along the nape of Julia's neck bristled, but the older socialite continued. "Besides, who said his donation was small? The new Sugar Falls Fire Department is going to have a steam room, a sauna and a state-of-the-art dispatch center thanks to us and Mr. Chatterson's charitable spirit."

How could he possibly have managed that? Perhaps he wasn't as poor as she'd initially thought. Nor was the

Sugar Falls Fire Department, if its sponsors were installing saunas in the building. Before she could think about this new revelation further, the man in question strode back into the ballroom.

"So, what did Charlie want?" Freckles asked him once the server dropped off another round of drinks.

Kane looked at Julia, then at the guests seated near their table. "Nothing that needs to be talked about here."

She was surprised that her normally nosy aunt and Cessy Walker, who made no secret of their vast wealth of town gossip, didn't follow up with more questions. Julia couldn't help but feel this was more than some social nuance she couldn't understand. But were they purposely keeping something from her?

Jonesy and Scooter Deets, the older cowboys Julia recognized from the café, were making their way over to the table when, out of nowhere, a boy who couldn't have been more than eighteen walked by their table and blinded them with the flash of his camera phone before scurrying toward the lobby.

"Damn," Kane said, then ran his fingers through hair that had started off the evening perfectly combed. He turned away from the table and took a few steps before pausing and returning to Julia's side. "You ready to get out of here?"

It was almost as though he was going to leave without her and then remembered he needed to give her a ride home. Something was wrong, and her stomach twisted in both disappointment and confusion. They'd been having such a great night up until now, and suddenly Kane was on edge. Her voice wobbled slightly when she said, "I guess so."

Kane grabbed her hand, and she tried to keep up with his long-legged strides as he steered them between tables and guests making their way to the dance floor. They passed Chief Wilcox so quickly, Julia was forced to turn back and give her a little wave goodbye. She saw Cessy in the center of the room, talking to Chief Cooper and pointing their way, but before she could ask Kane to slow down, she stumbled behind him.

He must have felt her slip, because he stopped only long enough to ask her if she was okay.

"Yes, but the skirt of my dress is too tight for me to take big steps, so I can't really keep up with you."

She couldn't be positive over the sound of the music, but she was pretty sure he'd made a growling sound in his throat before hauling her up against him again. By the time they made it to the resort's lobby, he had slowed his pace, but his face was set in stone-cold fury.

Julia's father had had a temper, and even though she wasn't good at reading men, she knew when to avoid someone angry. But she wasn't afraid of Kane. Despite the confusion twisting through her rib cage, she knew he wasn't angry with her, and she had a feeling that he shouldn't be alone right now.

She realized she'd left her wrap back at the table the moment they walked outside and the frigid mountain air hit her bare arms. Yet before they even made it to the valet stand, Kane had shrugged out of his tuxedo jacket and settled it over her shoulders.

Instead of waiting for the truck to be brought around, Kane grabbed his keys from the parking attendant and held Julia tightly against him as they crunched their way across the freshly fallen snow on the parking lot. Actually, they walked so far, they were no longer in the main parking lot, but in an empty area behind the service entrance.

Thanks to Julia's open-toed shoes, her feet were damp

and almost numb by the time Kane opened the passenger-side door for her. She waited for him to start the engine before she asked, "Do you want to talk about what happened in there?"

Kane's head was resting against the leather headrest, his eyes staring out the windshield as his wipers cleared off crescent shapes in the snow. "No."

"Do you want to be left alone?" It would be embarrassing and awkward for Julia to go back inside the lodge to find another ride, but she understood his need for solitude even when she didn't understand why he was upset.

"Yes, I want to be *left* alone, but I don't want to *be* alone. If that makes any sense."

"It makes perfect sense." Actually, none of this made any sense to Julia, but her heart was aching for whatever had caused the man this much pain. Since she didn't know how to fix it, the least she could do for him was stay by his side. What did normal people do in times like this? "Do you want to go somewhere and get a drink?"

"The last thing I need right now is a drink," Kane said.

"What do you need? I want to—" But before she could get the words out, his mouth silenced her.

Kane was lost. Right here in the annex parking lot behind the Snow Creek Lodge, he was absolutely lost. The second Julia had opened her lips to him, he'd been a complete goner. He curved his hand around her neck, pulling her face closer to his. She'd asked him what he needed and this was it.

He needed her. He needed to forget that he was once Legend Chatterson, and he needed to forget that Charlie, his agent, was still bugging him with assistant pitching coach offers and an insistence that he return to baseball.

He needed to forget that he couldn't hide from his former life forever.

Slowly he began to forget about all of that, because being with Julia was so mind-consuming he could think of nothing but touching her. He could deal with the consequences later, the rejection when she realized that he was some old washed-up has-been, completely out of her league. But right now, her hands were caressing his face, sliding down his neck and into his collar, and he thought that just maybe, for tonight, he could be with someone who didn't know about his old life and all the mistakes he'd made.

Sure, it was unfair not to disclose his inadequacies to Julia before he took her right here in the front seat of his truck. But it was also unfair the way she'd slipped his tuxedo jacket off her shoulders and was pressing her satin-covered breasts against his white dress shirt as she used her tongue to claim his mouth.

"Jules," he said, pulling back.

"Don't apologize."

"I'm not. I was going to say that if we don't go somewhere else, I'm going to end up taking you right here."

"In your truck?"

"Yes. In my truck. In the parking lot. With that dress pushed up around your waist."

She was still plastered against him, the center armrest between their hips the only thing keeping him from making good on the threat he'd meant to shock her back into her senses.

But instead of looking shocked, she simply said, "Technically, we aren't in the parking lot. And I've never had sex in a vehicle. Yet."

She rose up to her knees and pressed in closer to him, her lips resuming their quick work of making him lose what was left of his mind.

* * *

How long had she wondered about the feel of his hair? Would the other parts of his body—the ones she hadn't been able to stop thinking about since that night she'd found him painting her bathroom without his shirt—feel this good?

She had to find out. Right now.

Julia slid her fingers down under the collar of his white dress shirt, making her way through the buttons, only to be dismayed by the soft fabric of his white T-shirt underneath.

If only she had a pair of surgical shears to speed up the process. Perhaps in her eagerness, though, she'd come on too strong, because he moved his hands up to cradle her face, but pulled just far enough back to look at her. The only light was from the dim glow of the dashboard, yet she saw that Kane had a question in his eyes. She prayed he wasn't going to ask her if she'd lost all common sense. Clearly the answer to that was a resounding yes.

"Jules?"

"I love it when you call me that," she said, hoping he wasn't going to reject her for throwing herself at him.

He tilted his head to the side, his slightly swollen mouth grinning vaguely. "Why's that?"

"It doesn't sound so formal. I don't want to be formal with you anymore, Kane." She pushed forward to meet his lips, but after only seconds, he broke the kiss again.

"I don't want to be formal with you, either, Jules."

Her heart skipped a beat as a warm shiver spread through her. He groaned before shoving the center armrest up and pulling her onto his lap. If she'd thought his kisses had aroused her before, that was nothing compared to what his hands were doing to her. She felt the calluses on his work-roughened palms slip beneath the thin straps of her dress and gave a silent thanks that she'd forgone a bra since she didn't own a strapless one.

When his hands pulled her breasts free of the satin material, Julia couldn't remember what she was even giving thanks for. The coarseness of his fingertips couldn't mask the tenderness of his strokes as he brought her nipples to rock-hard peaks.

His tongue followed a similar pattern within the confines of her mouth, and she was forced to pull the hem of her dress up to her thighs so she could straddle him. His fingers moved away, and she gave a slight whimper at his withdrawal and the way the cool air lingered in his place. Then she realized he'd only adjusted his touch so that he could slide the rest of her dress over her waist and then her head.

She was wearing nothing but lace panties and a blush, and though she'd had sex only a handful of times with the college professor she'd briefly dated, she didn't want Kane to think she was a slow learner.

She reached for the hem of his T-shirt and lifted it off him, briefly breaking their joined lips. Kane paused and Julia, afraid he might get distracted or—worse—change his mind, grabbed his shoulders and pulled him toward her. Even if she hadn't been eager to feel his bare skin against hers, she needed to prove that she could be somewhat competent at this despite her limited experience.

It certainly felt more natural than riding a bike.

He lifted her hips slightly and settled her firmly onto his lap. She gasped at the sensation of the ridge inside his tuxedo pants pressed against her most intimate parts, and she wished she could wrap her legs around him, drawing him in closer.

"Are you sure?" he asked, and she wanted to giggle and scream in frustration at the same time. She was almost nude, nearly exposed and completely loving this reversal of her usual inhibitions. She'd never been more unsure of anything in her life. But she'd also never been as alive as she was now. She was an academic intellectual—a conventional person who did things by the book. Julia liked only things that made sense. And to her quivering body, Kane Chatterson made perfect sense. Besides, Julia Fitzgerald didn't quit. She wasn't stopping now.

"Please," she whispered.

He effortlessly lifted her and set her on the passenger seat facing him. Placing his fingers in the waistband of her panties, he worked the scrap of lace over her hips and down her legs. Then he ran his hand toward her left knee, pushed it up, leaned forward and kissed the sensitive flesh right above it. She would have clamped her thighs together if he hadn't been between them, his hands firmly on her waist and holding her in place. She was about to ask him what he was doing, but then his tongue touched the center of her heat. Julia threw back her head, her eyes closed in raw pleasure.

She'd never had sex like *this* before. It was one thing to read about this kind of thing in books, but no written definition could ever tell her how intoxicating it would be to feel the stubble from Kane Chatterson's strongly chiseled jaw rubbing against her most sensitive flesh. This was unlike any classroom she'd ever been in, and instead of taking notes, she was rocking her hips toward him. Silently begging for more.

"Not yet," Kane said, pulling his wallet out of his back pocket. She heard the rustling of plastic packaging. Then Kane shoved off his pants, and Julia barely had time to register how perfectly shaped his body was before he moved his hands under her hips and slid inside her depths.

"Kane," she said after only the third thrust. "I'm going to… I can't wait…"

He withdrew, but only partially. "Do you want me to slow down?"

"No. Yes. I don't know. I just want it to stay perfect like this."

"Aw, honey, you're perfect at everything you do."

"But it feels so good. I don't want it to be over yet."

"Don't worry." He smiled, then pushed himself in deeper, causing her to moan. "It doesn't ever have to be over."

He caught her next gasp with his mouth. When he thrust inside her again, she cried out, anchoring herself to him as the waves of pleasure crashed over her body.

"I thought you said it didn't have to be over?" Julia raised an eyebrow at Kane as he balanced himself between her trembling legs, trying to recover his breath. Despite the fact that he was usually so impatient and antsy, he'd never been one to rush sex. Yet the second he felt her release, he'd lost all control and hadn't been able to stop his own.

"I meant that we could keep going." His raspy voice sounded as though he'd made a hundred sprints around the bases. "Again. Later. After I recover a little."

"But it's never felt like that for me before."

"It's like warming up in the bull pen," he explained, pushing several blond strands away from her flushed face. Normally he liked her cute, swinging ponytail, but after seeing all the loose hair surrounding her face when she was calling out his name, he liked it down so much more. "You have to throw a few pitches to loosen you up and get the nerves out so that when you take the mound, you're ready to bring the heat."

"Is that a baseball reference?"

"Yes?" He tucked his chin and wrinkled his brow, hoping she wasn't offended. Did she think it was odd that he'd just compared sex to pitching? "I couldn't think of a more passionate sport to relate it to."

"I've never played many sports, but if what we did was just practice, I doubt I can handle a real game."

He let out his breath, along with a small chuckle. "Trust me, Captain Fitzgerald, you're more than ready for the big leagues."

"I don't know about that," she said, then blushed when she couldn't reach the discarded panties on the driver's-side floorboard. He sat up and handed them to her, along with her dress.

"So, what do we do now?" she asked, not attempting to hide the fact that she was blatantly checking him out while he wiggled his way back into his slacks. The woman was too honest and too curious for her own good.

What he wanted to say was that now they did the whole thing all over again. But slower this time. Too bad he was afraid to make the suggestion and have her laugh in his face. "Why are you asking me?"

She looked at the torn wrapper on the floor after pulling the satin over her head. "I was under the impression you were a bit more experienced in this kind of thing."

All it would take was one glance at the expiration date on that same wrapper to see that he'd been carrying the condom around for so long out of habit, he was just as out of experience as she was. They were lucky the stupid thing hadn't ripped. Although he could imagine worse things than having a baby with Dr. Smarty-Pants.

Whoa. He rubbed at his entire jawline. His brain was really getting ahead of itself with dangerous thoughts like that. He had no business thinking about any sort of future with her.

If he even wanted one. Oh God, he did. Maybe it was just the postcoital hormones talking, but he'd had sex with her only once and already he found himself thinking about a future with her. Yet the whole idea was impossible. Sooner or later, she'd figure it on her own, and all of this would come crashing down on him.

"What do *you* want to do now?" There, he'd put the ball back in her court. She bit her lip. "I've always been taught that practice makes perfect."

Something stirred in his belly, and it wasn't a lack of food. Was this what hope felt like?

"Given your opinions on failure, I bet you can't stand not being perfect at something." The corners of her mouth turned up, the same way they had when she'd been challenged to learn how to ride the tandem bike.

"I certainly like to get things right."

"Well, if you keep looking at me like that, you'll end up with a lot more practice than you've bargained for."

She traced her fingers along the scar on his shoulder, and he had to close his eyes briefly to remind himself not to let his impulses get ahead of things again. Maybe she knew exactly who he was, after all. And exactly what she was getting herself into.

"I wouldn't mind that," she said simply.

"Here?" He sounded like an overeager batboy sitting in the dugout for the first time.

"Maybe not *here*, exactly." She blushed again.

"We could go back to your place, but then we risk your neighbors seeing me parked in front of your house all night."

"*All* night?" Instead of seeing doubt, he recognized the dare in her eyes.

"Only if you want to become an expert at it."

"Do *you* have any neighbors you're worried about seeing us?" she asked.

"Not a single one," he responded. "But we might need to make a stop at Duncan's Market."

"Were you expecting to work up an appetite?" She grinned.

Kane was starting to like this confident and sassy side of Julia. It also helped ease his guilt to think that if she could make jokes, she wasn't having second thoughts. Yet. "Actually, I was going to buy more protection. That one from my wallet was a leftover from... Well, let's just say I haven't needed to stock up on those kinds of things in a long time."

"Oh." She blushed a little.

"If not, we can stop in at the Gas 'N' Mart. I'm sure Mrs. Marconi would love the firsthand gossip."

He was obviously teasing and expected her to voice an objection to anyone in Sugar Falls finding out they were involved romantically. Kane himself was uncertain how he felt about people knowing he and Julia Fitzgerald were involved as more than a contractor and a client. On the one hand, he now preferred living his life under the radar and detested the idea of anyone knowing his personal business. On the other hand, having someone as smart and successful as Julia by his side made him want to show off to the world. *See, I haven't made a total mess of my life.*

But Julia didn't respond, and at this hour, the market was probably closed anyway. He pulled the antique watch out of his pocket and clicked it open to look at the time. It was then that he realized he hadn't looked at the thing since he'd picked Julia up. Even with Charlie call-

ing him and the kid taking the picture, he hadn't been
overly antsy tonight.

Kane turned on the satellite radio, and B. B. King
crooned through his speakers about being home for
Christmas. They were both quiet as he drove through
town, the light dusting of recent snow making the holiday decorations stand out. He stopped by the minimart
at the gas station to pick up additional provisions—and
a box of Raisinets for her—and instead of avoiding eye
contact with the other late-night customers or the duck-
ing from the security cameras, Kane's chest puffed out
with satisfaction.

When they got to his house, an old remodeled barn
nestled near Sprinkle Creek, he led her to the upstairs
loft, which he'd converted into a master bedroom and
bath equipped with more modern amenities than the new
Sugar Falls Fire Department facility he'd been tricked
into financing. Then, in an effort to be a good host, he
went along very willingly when she pulled him into the
shower with her. They made love against the white mar-
ble tile, and then again in his king-size bed.

The following morning, the sun's pinkish light spilled
into his wall of steel-framed windows, giving Julia's pale
skin a glow as she rose above him in a steady rhythm,
bringing him to the edge of ecstasy and then sending
him over.

When she collapsed beside him on the bed, he stroked
his hand from her shoulder to her hip, outlining the con-
tours of her curves. He kissed her and said, "I finally feel
as if I'm on an even playing field with you."

"What do you mean?" She grinned.

"I'm not like you, Jules." He brought his fingers to
her hair and tapped lightly at her temple. "I don't have

any of this. You're so smart and so successful, and I'm neither of those things."

"How can you say you're not smart?" She sat up, taking the pale blue sheet with her. "You're brilliant when it comes to measurements and calculating materials and envisioning what a finished home should look like."

"Brilliant? Hardly. I barely graduated high school with a C-minus average."

"You have ADHD, not a low IQ."

He shook his head. "It might as well be the same thing."

"No, Kane. It's actually the opposite. I wish I could give you a baseball analogy because I know how much you relate to those, but I'm not familiar with that world. Yet. So I'll give you a driving one instead." He didn't want to point out that she didn't have much more experience with driving, either. "When you have ADHD, your brain is like a race car. A high-performance race car. It works so much faster and more powerfully than most normal brains. The problem, though, is that your race car brain has brakes made for Aiden and Caden's tandem bicycle. So when it's time to slow down or to make a turn, your brakes aren't sufficient, and you spin off the road. The ability to perform is there. You simply have to address the mechanics of it all to get it to run smoothly. Does that make sense?"

"I think so." He looked up at his motionless industrial-size ceiling fan. Suddenly his life felt as calm and as still as the blades on that fan. He had to find his own brakes, his own light switch to turn his spinning engine on and off. "Nobody's ever explained it to me that way."

"Good. Because I know what I'm talking about. I'm an expert, remember?" Julia leaned over to kiss him, but before he could pull her on top of him, a knock sounded on the door. "Do you get a lot of company on Sunday mornings?" she asked.

"I don't get a lot of company anytime," he replied. "Maybe it's someone for you."

She gulped and pulled her sheet up tighter. So much for the sassy expert. Kane laughed at her rediscovered social discomfort. "It could be Drew or Luke with the twins."

Julia let out a small squeak and dove for her dress, which lay crumpled on the floor. Kane chuckled and pulled on his slacks from the night before. He didn't bother with a shirt, because whoever was knocking at this time of day knew better than to expect a warm and friendly welcome.

Sure enough, when he swung open the door, the person on the other side made him feel anything but warm and friendly. "Erica? What are you doing here?"

Chapter Twelve

"**I** was in the neighborhood and thought I'd stop by." Julia heard the visitor's words as she walked down the loft steps. He glanced at her before looking outside at whoever this Erica woman was. "Aren't you going to invite me in? I've missed you, Kane."

That voice sounded more than friendly. It didn't take a dating authority to recognize that the sultry tone was flirtatious in nature. And intimate. It also was apparent that whoever was on the other side of that door was someone Kane didn't want Julia to see. She braced herself for the nausea sure to come. The same thing had happened after she'd found out that Professor Mosely was married.

Thank goodness she'd resisted the urge to throw on one of his flannel shirts and pulled her evening gown over her head instead. She might look a mess—perhaps even like she'd been up all night making love—but at least she was in her own clothing. Embarrassed. Potentially disgraced. Possibly even lied to. But she owned it.

"I'd better get going," Julia whispered from behind Kane.

He glanced at her quickly. "No. I don't want you to leave."

"Who's that?" the woman outside asked.

"That's none of your business, Erica. How did you find out where I lived?"

"I'm a reporter, Kane. I find things out."

Julia let out a breath. If the lady was someone important to Kane—like a wife or a girlfriend—his address wouldn't be a secret. Still, Julia wasn't convinced Erica's surprise arrival was anything but ominous.

This situation wasn't good. Why was a reporter standing outside, talking to Kane as if they had some sort of close relationship? At least, the woman was speaking that way. Kane's tone indicated he wanted nothing to do with this Erica person, which was good as far as eliminating the notion that he was cheating on another woman with Julia. However, his tone also indicated that he was hiding out from something or someone. And that was a secret he hadn't shared with Julia.

She'd finally opened up to Kane, letting down her defenses and forgetting the lesson she'd painfully learned as a second-year med student. Yet she was now in danger of finding out that the man she'd let get close to her wasn't who he seemed.

Pushing back at the irrational doubts throbbing in her head, Julia reminded herself that Kane was different than Stewart Mosely. The older professor had been an infatuation, someone in a position of authority over her who'd taken advantage of her naïveté.

Kane hadn't done that, had he? Surely, their lovemaking last night—and this morning—wouldn't have been the most intense and physically overwhelming she'd ever experienced if he'd been holding back a piece of himself.

Julia wracked her brain for red flags that she'd missed these past two months, but it was difficult to concentrate with the obnoxious odor of Erica's heavily applied perfume floating into the house. She'd felt like a failure after the whole fiasco with Professor Mosely because when she'd realized her mistake, she hadn't *wanted* to salvage their relationship.

With Kane, she didn't even know if there was a relationship to salvage. Julia pulled her hair into as neat a ponytail as she could manage and told herself she wasn't going to waste any more time not knowing.

"Hi." She pushed herself under Kane's arm and stuck out her hand. "I'm Julia."

"Oh my," the stunning brunette said, taking a step back instead of meeting the offered handshake. "The picture didn't lie. I didn't know you'd moved on so quickly, Kane."

"It's been two years, Erica. And I moved on the second I woke up from surgery and found out you'd spent the night with Arturo Dominguez."

"Babe." Erica tsk-tsked. "I was only trying to get the story. You'll never have any idea what it's like to be a female sportscaster in a man's world."

What picture? And what story? The throbbing in her brain intensified as she tried to make sense of the crumbs of information being tossed her way.

Kane shoved a hand through his hair. "Don't act like there was some sort of inside scoop. The only story was that he ruined your boyfriend's career when he rushed the mound with that baseball bat."

"He didn't ruin your career, Kane. You were getting too old for the pros, anyway. It was time to hang up your glove and get into coaching. Charlie said you've had several offers from some of the top pro teams. Why haven't you taken any of them?"

"Is that how you found me?" Kane cursed. "You got my address from Charlie?"

"Who's Charlie?" Julia whispered, latching onto the name she recognized from last night.

"Charlie's my agent."

Kane had an agent? An agent for what? It had something to do with baseball and sportscasters and taking a new offer. Unfortunately, Julia didn't want to stand out here in the freezing air, trying patiently to sort this all out. Nor did she want this woman as an audience when Kane explained who he was and what he'd been keeping from her.

Julia hated secrets. They made her feel ignorant and powerless. She relied on knowledge, not intuition. Facts, not gut feelings. A long time ago, her instincts had been right about Professor Mosely, and she had only herself to blame for not paying better attention.

As frustrated as she was with Kane for not opening up to her sooner, she couldn't very well fault him for avoiding questions she hadn't thought to ask in the first place. He hadn't lied to her, as far as she knew. And he seemed just as upset about this woman's unannounced arrival as Julia was. She had no idea what was going on, but she knew that if the situations were reversed and Julia was even the slightest bit uncomfortable, Kane would be the first one to jump into the middle of things and protect her.

So she decided to do the same for him by giving him a polite way to excuse himself. "You know, I hate to cut this short, but I'm going home so I can check on Mr. Donut."

"Crap. I forgot about him. I'll go get my keys."

Kane backed away from the door, and Julia stepped into his place, prepared to ask the woman who exactly she was. But the words never came, because, in the end, she wanted to hear it from Kane. He owed her that.

Out of the corner of her eye, she saw him take the steps two at a time. He was already on his way downstairs, his keys and a jacket in hand, when Erica asked, "Who's Mr. Donut?"

"My dog," Julia replied.

"Our dog," Kane said at the same time, his declaration causing goose bumps to rise along her skin. He put his arm around her waist.

"He's still *ours*, right?" Kane whispered into her hair, causing a shiver to vibrate down her spine.

"Depends on who *you* are, Kane Chatterson." Julia's response was not a whisper.

"I'm still me, Jules," he said, the endearing nickname flooding her with more confusion and uncertainty. "No matter what she says or what you find out, just keep that in mind."

"Oh my God," Erica clapped a well-manicured hand to her cheek. "Please don't tell me that your little girlfriend from this little town has no idea you're Legend Chatterson."

Legend? There was that nickname again.

"Would someone like to tell me what I'm missing here?" Julia asked, feeling slightly empowered by Kane's announcement that they shared a dog and his tight grip of the car keys she was trying to pry out of his closed fist.

"I will," Kane said. "Just as soon as my ex-girlfriend leaves."

"She's your *ex*?" Okay, so that revelation took some of the sting out of Julia's growing frustration.

"You mean you don't know who I am, either?" Erica's bright white smile reminded Julia of a shark documentary she'd once seen in an oceanography course.

Julia glanced at the woman's wrap dress and Louboutin shoes, neither of which were appropriate for this weather. Her airbrushed makeup and perfectly curled hair looked professionally done and more suited to a fancy cocktail party. But she didn't care what this woman looked like. Nobody made Julia Fitzgerald feel unintelligent. "Should I?"

"Only if you haven't been living in a bubble the past two years, completely unaware of one of the biggest pro baseball scandals of the twenty-first century. My news station reported on it nonstop for twenty-eight days straight." Erica looked at Kane's stony expression, probably ensuring she had a captive audience, before continuing. "Allow me to fill you in, cupcake."

Living in a bubble? The words were like a slap across Julia's face because that's precisely what she'd been doing these past months.

"First of all—" Julia rose to her full height in her strappy evening shoes and squared her shoulders, her years of poise lessons coming in handy "—it's *Doctor*, not *cupcake*. Second of all, no, I don't have a clue who you are because I don't sit in front of my television set all day, watching newscasters speculate about sports scandals. I'm a neurosurgeon, and I'm too busy saving lives instead of trying to wreak havoc on everyone else's."

Clearly Erica wasn't used to having to back down, because she placed her hands on her hips and shot back, "It doesn't matter how many lives you save, cupcake. Kane Chatterson was once considered the MVP of the single world. You're just another stat on his score card."

The woman turned on her designer heel and made a regal retreat to a nondescript rental car. As Erica opened the door, she looked over her shoulder and called out,

"When you're ready to return to the real world, Kane, give me a call."

"Not a chance," Kane said, pulling Julia in even tighter.

As Erica's car kicked up dirt and gravel, Julia's evening bag vibrated on the entry table where she must have left it last night.

"Did you see it, Sug?" Freckles asked the second Julia answered the phone.

"See what?"

"Your picture with Kane is all over the news. He's got his arm around you, and you're all cozied up. I think the word the reporter used was *canoodling*. Don't that beat all?"

"What picture are you talking about, Aunt Freckles?"

"The one that kid snapped last night. I followed him to the bathroom, but Cessy told me I couldn't go inside to make a scene. Chief Cooper went in there to reason with the teen, but the thing had already been posted all over social media. Then Commodore Russell flushed the poor kid's phone down the toilet and all hell broke loose."

"Who's Commodore Russell?" Julia asked, then shook her head, keeping the phone to her ear as she turned toward the man hovering beside her. "Wait. That's not important. Who are *you*, Kane?"

"Did you go home with Kane, Sug?" Freckles asked. "Put him on."

"He can't talk right now," she replied, then gasped at her inadvertent admission. "I'll call you back later," Julia told her aunt, then tapped the red end button.

"I'm guessing that was Freckles?"

"You're guessing right. Now tell me what's going on. Who are you, Kane Chatterson?"

"You haven't told her?" A voice came from the cell

phone and Julia realized that instead of hanging up, she'd actually put the thing on speaker.

"No, Freckles, I thought she knew," Kane said. "It wasn't like everyone else in town wasn't broadcasting it everywhere I went."

"Knew what?" Julia was cold, she'd barely had any sleep last night and she was starting to get hungry. And if she didn't get some answers soon, she'd be trembling with anger.

"I'll explain everything when we get in the car."

"I'm not getting in any car with you until you tell me what's going on."

"You're taking the car?" Freckles asked through the speaker. "Wait until I tell Cessy and Kylie. He must be serious about you, Sug, if he's taking you out in the car."

"I simply grabbed the wrong keys, Freckles. Your niece will call you back later." Kane took the phone from Julia's hand and really disconnected the call this time. "We should probably go check on Mr. Donut."

Right. Their dog. Julia followed him past his truck, over to the building she'd assumed was some sort of equestrian stable when they'd driven up last night. He punched in a code on the keypad, and when the electric door rolled open, she saw the building was actually a garage.

The Bronco was parked to the left, where there was a workshop and what looked to be an entire mechanic's bay. To the right was a perfectly reconditioned blue Chevy truck, the license plate boasting the year 1952. Next to that was some sort of green muscle car Julia recognized from a Steve McQueen movie her dad used to watch.

"You restore cars, too?" she asked.

"Yeah," he said as though this was yet another thing about him that was clearly obvious. Julia had just done all sorts of intimate things with the man only to wake up this morning to find out she hadn't really known anything about him.

"But all of these must be worth a lot of money." Even someone who'd just bought her first car a few months ago understood the value of a classic automobile.

"Yep." He turned to look at her.

"Like, a whole lot of money."

Kane lifted a brow. "Is it a problem if I'm not some poor small-town contractor?"

Just then, several alerts pinged from Kane's pants pocket, and he pulled out his own cell phone.

"Aren't you Mr. Popular all of a sudden," Julia said.

"Everyone in town is trying to warn me about the picture online," he replied, a frown deeply etched in his face. Julia hated that frown. It had been there last night when they'd left the gala, and she'd put in a lot of intense physical effort to make him forget about whatever had bothered him.

And judging from the way his phone was repeatedly vibrating, a lot of other people didn't want him upset, either.

So everyone knew about Kane's career and his ex-girlfriend and his car collection. Had she been the only one left in Sugar Falls who was completely in the dark?

She put her palm out. "Give me the keys."

"Let me drive you home. We can talk about it on the way."

"I'm not going anywhere with you. Either give me the keys, or I'll call for a taxi."

"This is Sugar Falls. We don't have taxis. Sometimes Elaine Marconi's sister will use her own car for cab fares, but you don't really want everyone in town gossiping about you spending the night here, do you?"

Her response was to keep her hand extended as she glared at him.

"Jules, it's a sixty-eight Mustang GT. You know what you said about my brain being a superfast race car? The engine in this thing puts it to shame."

Julia gave him a dark look. "Luckily, I know how to slow things down."

Watching the way she peeled out of his driveway in his prized muscle car, Kane knew she was furious. And he couldn't blame her. Julia thought he'd kept this all a secret from her. Technically, he hadn't hidden anything from her, but he hadn't been quick to parade his disastrous past in front of her, either.

He reminded himself that she'd grown up sheltered. That a woman like her was used to things being laid out in black-and-white terms. All he needed was five minutes to explain things to the woman he wanted to spend the rest of his life with...

Oh God. It was true. He wanted to spend the rest of his life with Dr. Smarty-Pants, who'd looked as though she was going to split the second Erica had shown up. Not that any explanation he had would prevent Julia from laughing at what an idiot he'd been to think she could possibly feel the same way about him. What a mess he'd made of this, too.

His gut twisted and his fingers twitched. It was too much to hope for Julia not to dump him, but did she have to do it while gunning the V-8 engine he'd so patiently restored?

Then he replayed her words in his mind and recalled that she didn't break up with him. At least not in so many words. Kane looked at the other two vehicles parked in his garage.

Should he go after her, or should he give his impulses time to simmer down?

He went back into his house to grab his cell phone and another set of car keys—just in case. Then he called the one relative that was professionally obligated not to laugh at him.

His brother-in-law Drew picked up on the second ring. Kane explained the situation, the words tumbling out in a rush as he described the confrontation with Erica and Julia's departure. "Now Julia thinks I lied to her about my past and I need you to tell me how to convince a hardheaded woman how to give me a second chance."

"I heard that," his sister yelled in the background.

Kane let out a breath. "So much for doctor-patient privilege."

"You're not my patient," Drew reasoned with his calm psychologist voice. "Now tell me again what happened with Julia."

Kane stood outside his truck, flipping the keys around his finger as he told his brother-in-law—and his sister, who had obviously convinced her husband to put the call on speaker—what had happened with Julia this morning. Of course, he did leave out some of the more personal details, but the story took long enough that he felt like he should switch to Bluetooth and get Drew's advice while he followed Julia back to her house.

"Do you love her?" Drew asked.

"Who? Julia?" Kane put his truck in Drive.

"Of course Julia, you weenie," Kylie shouted loud enough to wake one of the babies who then began crying.

He'd thought he'd loved Erica, even imagined they'd end up married. But looking back on their relationship, her betrayal hadn't run as deep as the surgical scar on his shoulder. He'd been too busy mourning his career to give his ex-girlfriend a second thought. But Julia? Hell, losing her would do more damage than a team of doctors, coaches and meddling family members could ever repair.

"God, I really do." Saying the words out loud brought Kane a sense of calm. "Please tell me that's not the stupidest thing ever?"

"Do you feel like it's stupid?" Drew asked.

"Only if she doesn't love me back."

"Have you thought about asking her?"

"So she could laugh in my face?" Kane said, then took a left onto Snowflake Boulevard, already knowing he was willing to take that risk.

"Do you ever think you worry too much about losing?"

"Do you ever think you could just give me some advice or at least a brotherly pep talk instead of asking me all these rhetorical questions? You know what, never mind. I already figured it out for myself."

Kane disconnected the call while Drew was still chuckling.

And his brother-in-law had a good point, even if he hadn't said it directly. Kane hated to lose.

In fact, Julia was right when she'd once told him that he didn't like trying something if there was a chance he'd fail at it. Hell, she was right about a lot of things. Julia hated failure as much as he did, yet she was the opposite and would throw herself at a challenge, determined to become the best at it. Even if she hadn't wanted to do it—like going along with her aunt's makeover and dating plan.

Therefore, if Kane didn't want to lose her, he needed to convince Julia that he was a challenge worth taking on.

But just to be on the safe side, he stopped off at the

bakery and grabbed a bag of doughnuts for their dog because he needed all the backup he could get.

When he pulled up to the house on Pinecone Court, he was relieved to see his classic Mustang parked behind the MINI Cooper.

He knocked on the door, rocking back on his heels while he waited for her to answer. He probably would've had to wait a lot longer if Mr. Donut hadn't pressed his wet nose against the glass-paned windows in the entryway and seen the white bakery bag before barking like crazy.

Probably figuring out that the dog wouldn't calm down until he got his treats, Julia finally opened the door. She was still in her sexy evening gown and, even with all the creases caused by it spending the night forgotten on his bedroom floor, the sight of her froze his vocal cords.

"You must've come for these," she said holding out his keys.

He shook his head. "You can keep the car."

"Then would you mind giving those doughnuts to the dog before you leave so he'll stop making all this noise?"

"I know you're upset about what happened this morning," he said, holding up his free palm to stop her from closing the door. "But it wasn't like I purposely kept anything from you. Plus, all that stuff was from my past. It's not who I am anymore."

She crossed her arms over her chest and said, "Don't you think who we were in our past defines who we become?"

"You sound like my brother-in-law, Drew."

"Stop getting off-topic, Kane. Just tell me the truth. You were a professional baseball player?"

"Yes. A pitcher. I was drafted straight out of high

school and played in the minors for a couple of years before being called up to the majors."

"Were you good?"

"What kind of question is that?"

"It's just a question. I've come to the conclusion that I haven't been asking enough of those where you're concerned."

"Yes." He shifted from one foot to the other. "I was good."

"Is that why people call you Legend?"

"I guess."

"Now's not the time to be modest," she said. "Tell me why they call you Legend."

"I won the award for best pitcher in the league four years in a row. Which my dad never lets me forget, considering he won it only twice."

"Wait," she frowned. "Your father is a baseball star, too?"

"Well, he's a team manager now. He doesn't play anymore himself."

"What about you? Why aren't you playing baseball now?"

"You saw my shoulder," he said. "You also touched it, kissed it, rested your leg on it when—"

"I'm familiar with your shoulder, Kane." A crimson heat stole up her cheeks, and he was glad he'd sidetracked the conversation long enough to remind her of what they'd already shared. "But your ex-girlfriend mentioned something about a scandal, so I'm trying to figure out if that event was responsible for your drastic change in careers."

"At least you know that she is my ex-girlfriend. As in, very ex. A long-time-ago ex. A no-idea-she-was-going-to-show-up-out-of-the-blue ex."

"Yeah, I got that impression when half the population of Sugar Falls practically launched its own form of an emergency broadcast to warn you she was in town."

"I just didn't want you to think there was anything between me and her. Or that I would ever sleep with you if I wasn't completely free and available."

"We can talk about you sleeping with me after you tell me this baseball story," she said, not moving an inch, let alone inviting him inside.

Man, Julia would've been just as good a prosecuting attorney as she was a surgeon. "A couple of years ago, I was pitching in game six of the division series. We were up three to two, and there was a runner on second. Their designated hitter was at bat and hoping to set a home run record that night. But I walked him."

"Like, on purpose?"

"There's no more, buddy," he said to the dog as he brushed the sugar off his hands. "Yes, on purpose. A pitcher does that when there's a risk of someone scoring. The batter doesn't get an RBI and we stack the bases, which gives us a chance of making more outs."

"You're forgetting I don't speak baseball."

"Basically, the hitter got pissed that I walked him, and he charged the mound. That means he ran at me because he wanted to fight. But he brought his bat with him. He managed to get in a few solid blows to my shoulder before the dugouts cleared and the rest of the teams joined in. Supposedly it was one of the biggest brawls in televised history, and the news stations and broadcasters still refer to it as Brawlgate."

"What happened to the other guy? The one who hit you with a bat?"

"Arturo Dominguez? He was fined and suspended for a year. He's playing for a team in LA now."

"That's the guy you mentioned when you were talking to Erica."

"Yes."

"And she slept with him? While you were in surgery?"

"You heard her. She wanted to get the story."

Julia shook her head. "Tough crowd you used to run with."

"Nah. They weren't all bad."

"Then why not go back? Not as a player, but as a coach. It sounds like your dad and agent think you could."

"And be reminded of what I lost?"

"No. To be reminded of what you could give other players."

"I don't know. I never had the patience to coach. When I was pitching, I could focus out there because I was on my own little island. All I had to concentrate on was the ball in my hand going into the catcher's mitt."

"Do you miss it?"

"Baseball? Yeah. A little. Alex Russell and Luke Gregson talked me into umpiring a few Little League games last season. It was a nice balance, to be able to work on houses and then go to the ball field once or twice a week."

She looked him up and down, as if she were taking it all in. Taking him all in. And she still hadn't closed the door on his face.

"So, can we move on to the talk about us sleeping together?" he asked.

Instead of answering, Julia laughed and brushed by him before sitting down on her porch step. Hmm. Maybe he didn't like this sassy, confident Julia after all. Not when he was left wondering what was going through that brain of hers. The dog waddled beside her and rolled onto his back, sticking his stubby legs in the air as she rubbed its belly.

He took the smiling expression on her face as a good sign. But he would remain in suspense until he knew for certain that Julia felt at least something for him. "What are you thinking?" he asked.

"I'm thinking that I have a dog named Mr. Donut and that I just slept with a man named The Legend."

"Not *The*. Just *Legend*."

She rolled her eyes, then glanced back at him. "I'm still trying to wrap my head around all this new information I should've realized from the very beginning. I can't stand not knowing things."

"Yeah, I've been getting that feeling."

"Do you? I had no idea you were a famous baseball player. I had no idea Mr. Donut didn't belong to you." She was ticking off items on her fingers. "I had no idea that junky old Bronco of yours was a classic and probably worth as much as my MINI Cooper."

"You thought my Bronco was junky?"

"Kane, focus." She motioned for him to join her while the dog plopped between them. "What I'm trying to say is that I like knowledge. Sure, I could've found out most of that information with a simple internet search, and I'm annoyed with myself for being the last to know. But the thing I'm still trying to process—the thing nobody else can tell me—is how *you* feel."

"How I feel about what?"

"About me!"

"I'm crazy about you." He shot up and paced in front of her. "Stupid, mad, crazy about you."

"Don't say *stupid*. You're not stupid."

"Maybe not. But I have one more confession."

She tilted her head. "What else could you possibly confess?"

He immediately sat back down. "I knew about your man list before you ever brought it up."

Julia's hand flew to her mouth. "You saw that thing?"

"It was on your desk, in that picture you sent me with the tile samples. I hated the thought of you going out with some loser and thought I could steer you away from that. Plus, it helped remind me that you were so out of my league, the only criterion I met was my closet full of flannel shirts."

She started laughing. "You should've seen the first draft. It was all about you. Besides, I don't need some silly list to tell me that I love you, Kane."

He put a finger under her chin and looked into her eyes, not sure he'd heard correctly. "You love me?"

"Even before I knew you had an entirely different life before me, I loved everything about you." His fingers moved along her face, but he remained silent, unable to talk around the lump rising in his throat. "I love your quiet brooding and your impatient knee that jiggles whenever you're nervous. I love the way you know exactly what I want to buy or eat or drink and have it here at my house waiting for me before I even have to ask for it. I love the way you clean up after me because you require a clutter-free work zone. I love the way you negotiate with salespeople and take in wandering animals, then pass them off to someone else."

"In my defense—" Kane scratched the basset hound between his floppy ears "—Mr. Donut was making himself at home here."

"Only because you would feed him baked goods every morning." She pushed playfully at his arm.

Kane took her hand and kissed her palm. "Tell me what else you love."

"I especially love the way you look in those sexy flannel shirts."

"I knew you were a smart woman."

"I think you've been the smart one, Kane Chatterson. You steered me straight into your arms."

"I love you, Julia. Just you."

Epilogue

Six Months Later

"Sug, you're supposed to slice the strawberries," Freckles said. "Not make jam out of them."

Julia hadn't quite mastered the technique. Yet. But she was getting close. Her aunt demonstrated how to use the knife crosswise along the cutting board as the Dixieland Jazz Band played a catchy tune from the gazebo in Town Square Park.

And because her aunt didn't do anything small, the sign for the Cowgirl Up Café's booth was almost as big as the Shortcake Festival banner strung up across Snowflake Boulevard. The town's main street was closed off so the townspeople and tourists could freely roam amongst the vendors and the carnival-style atmosphere.

"I can't believe that good-looking man of yours built you that fancy gourmet kitchen and you still don't know what to do in it." Freckles tsk-tsked.

"Oh she knows what to do in it all right," Kane said as he walked up, Mr. Donut on the leash beside him. Julia blushed and Freckles threw a strawberry at him, which he caught. "I just do most of the cooking for us."

Which was true. Kane hadn't officially moved into her house yet, but he spent more nights there than he did at his own place. She waved at Chief Wilcox, who was walking across the street, holding hands with Marcus Weston.

"Kane." Cessy Walker materialized from across the street. "I'm so glad you're finally making more social appearances around town, because we could really use you to drum up business at the Chamber of Commerce's kissing booth."

Kane let out a bark of laughter. "No way. And don't even try to manipulate me into volunteering again."

"But Alex Russell and his hunky dad Vic were supposed to take this time slot and they sent over the commodore instead." Cessy pointed to the stocky eighty-year-old man with a gray crew cut and a toothpick clenched tightly between his teeth. Sitting on a stool with his arms crossed over his barrel chest, the senior Russell looked like he'd rather punch someone than kiss them. "And we're set up right next to Maxine Cooper's cookie stand. How can we compete with that?"

"I'll tell you what—" Kane pulled out his wallet and peeled off a few large bills. "—consider this my contribution."

Freckles rewarded his generosity with a paper bowl loaded down with strawberry shortcake and Kane winked at Julia, making her insides feel as creamy as the whipped topping he was licking off his plastic spoon.

A dinging bell sounded right before one of the Gregson twins yelled, "Look out, Uncle Kane!" Julia held her breath as the tandem bike narrowly missed running over her boyfriend's toes.

"Why did I start venturing out in public again?" he asked her.

"Because you love me," Julia replied. "And because we both agreed to put ourselves out there socially."

"I think I'd agree to just about anything for you." He rolled his eyes, but he couldn't hide that smirk of his.

"Hey, Coach Chatterson," the starting pitcher from the Sugar Falls High School baseball team said as he approached the booth with a crowd of teenagers. "I've been working on that curveball you taught me in May."

Julia smiled to herself as she turned to scoop up more strawberries for the new orders. Kane was still doing remodels, but he was also getting back into the sport he loved.

"Kane Chatterson," Freckles scolded. "Don't you dare feed that mutt any more of my shortcake. He'll get a bellyache from all the sugar."

When Julia turned around to remind him that Mr. Donut was only supposed to be eating the special weight control food the vet prescribed, she saw Kane down on one knee, their dog licking the bowl next to him.

"Oh my gosh," her aunt squealed loud enough to draw a crowd and it was then that Julia—and everyone else in town—saw the glittering engagement ring he was holding in his hand.

"Captain Julia Fitzgerald." Kane's voice shook as several people held up their smartphones and began snapping pictures of Legend Chatterson. She sucked in a breath, not caring about the tears filling up her eyes. Julia couldn't believe he was doing this here, in such a public place, as though he had something to prove to her. Or himself. "Will you please agree to marry me so we can get the hell out of here and go home to plan our elopement?"

"Of course she will," Freckles said, before Julia shot her the stay out of it look she'd been practicing lately.

"Of course I will," Julia echoed the words before Kane slid the not-so-discreet ring on her finger.

"I love you," he whispered so that only she could hear. And as she wrapped her arms around him, she decided that she couldn't wait to get him home. All alone.

* * * * *

Don't miss Alex Russell's story,

A FAMILY UNDER THE STARS

the next installment in Christy Jeffries'
new series
SUGAR FALLS, IDAHO
On sale March 2017, wherever Mills & Boon
books and ebooks are sold!

MILLS & BOON®

Cherish™

EXPERIENCE THE ULTIMATE RUSH OF FALLING IN LOVE

A sneak peek at next month's titles...

In stores from 12th January 2017:

- **The Sheikh's Convenient Princess** – Liz Fielding *and* **His Pregnant Courthouse Bride** – Rachel Lee
- **The Billionaire of Coral Bay** – Nikki Logan *and* **Baby Talk & Wedding Bells** – Brenda Harlen

In stores from 26th January 2017:

- **Her First-Date Honeymoon** – Katrina Cudmore *and* **Falling for the Rebound Bride** – Karen Templeton
- **The Unforgettable Spanish Tycoon** – Meg Maxwell *and* **Her Sweetest Fortune** – Stella Bagwell

---

Just can't wait?
Buy our books online a month before they hit the shops!
www.millsandboon.co.uk

Also available as eBooks.

MILLS & BOON®

EXCLUSIVE EXTRACT

Sheikh Ibrahim al-Ansari must find a bride,
and quickly… Thankfully he has the perfect
convenient princess in mind—his new assistant,
Ruby Dance!

Read on for a sneak preview of
THE SHEIKH'S CONVENIENT PRINCESS
by Liz Fielding

'Can I ask if you are in any kind of relationship?' he
persisted.

'Relationship?'

'You are on your own—you have no ties?'

He was beginning to spook her and must have realised
it because he said, 'I have a proposition for you, Ruby,
but if you have personal commitments…' He shook his
head as if he wasn't sure what he was doing.

'If you're going to offer me a package too good to
refuse after a couple of hours I should warn you that it
took Jude Radcliffe the best part of a year to get to that
point and I still turned him down.'

'I don't have the luxury of time,' he said, 'and the
position I'm offering is made for a temp.'

'I'm listening.'

'Since you have done your research, you know that
I was disinherited five years ago.'

She nodded. She thought it rather harsh for a one-off

incident but the media loved the fall of a hero and had gone into a bit of a feeding frenzy.

'This morning I received a summons from my father to present myself at his birthday majlis.'

'You can go home?'

'If only it were that simple. A situation exists which means that I can only return to Umm al Basr if I'm accompanied by a wife.'

She ignored the slight sinking feeling in her stomach. Obviously a multimillionaire who looked like the statue of a Greek god—albeit one who'd suffered a bit of wear and tear—would have someone ready and willing to step up to the plate.

'That's rather short notice. Obviously, I'll do whatever I can to arrange things, but I don't know a lot about the law in—'

'The marriage can take place tomorrow. My question is, under the terms of your open-ended brief encompassing "whatever is necessary", are you prepared to take on the role?'

Don't miss
THE SHEIKH'S CONVENIENT PRINCESS
By Liz Fielding

Available February 2017
www.millsandboon.co.uk

Give a 12 month subscription to a friend today!

Call Customer Services
0844 844 1358[*]

or visit
millsandboon.co.uk/subscription: